GLITTER

Elise Noble

Published by Undercover Publishing Limited

ISBN: 978-1-912888-12-2

Edited by Amanda Ann Larson and Nikki Mentges

Cover design by Elise Noble

www.undercover-publishing.com

www.elise-noble.com

All that is gold does not glitter.
- *J. R. R. Tolkien*

CHAPTER 1

"*NYET*! GET OFF there."

The dog ignored Ana until she made a grab for it, then the four-legged fiend leapt back, knocking a box of eggs off the counter with one front paw as it did so. Ana stretched for the eggs and caught them, but she forgot about the flour in her other hand. The bag hit the floor with a quiet *thump* and exploded, covering every surface in the kitchen with its contents, Ana and her not-quite-three-year-old daughter included.

"*Gavno!*"

Despite the fact that she lived in America now, Virginia to be precise, Ana still cursed in Russian half the time. But quietly so Tabitha didn't copy. The little girl was meant to be starting preschool soon, something that left Ana twitchy, and being a mom was hard enough without getting hauled in by the principal to apologise for your child's language.

A cake. She'd just wanted to make a cake. The perky blonde woman on Cooking Channel managed it with no trouble at all, but Ana's previous attempts had been flat, burned, and squidgy respectively. And now there was fucking flour everywhere. She grabbed a roll of paper towel and began wiping, and that was when she smelled smoke.

"*Eto pizdets!*"

Ana's boyfriend, Sam, had insisted on having a fire extinguisher in the kitchen, which said a lot about either his sense of paranoia or his faith in Ana's culinary skills. Since they'd practically lived together in Russia four years ago and he'd pretended to enjoy her charred offerings several times a week back then, she suspected the latter.

But whatever, today she was grateful for his foresight as she grabbed the extinguisher and blasted what was left of the caramel sauce into a cloud of vapour.

Just as someone knocked on the door.

Ana stiffened. For a person to get to the apartment door, they'd have to get past the external door first. Which meant they either had a key fob, or they'd bypassed the system. Ana could do that in a heartbeat—indeed, she had many times in many apartment blocks, and on none of those occasions was it to wish the occupants a happy birthday. Actually, there was that one time she'd posed as a florist and—

Forget that. Where the hell was her gun?

In another life, she'd kept two pistols on her at all times, but since her goal when she came to America had been to be normal—to fit in and have Tabby grow up like a regular kid—the concealed-carry holsters now lived in her gun safe. Probably she should have locked all the guns in there too, but old habits died hard. Still, she only carried one pistol now. And since the damn thing kept slipping in the waistband of her yoga pants, she'd put it on top of the fridge, out of Tabby's reach, and now it too was covered in a sticky mess of flour and firefighting foam.

Ana wiped it on her apron and ran into the hallway,

just in time to see Tabby drag open the front door. How, you ask? She'd stood on the fucking dog to reach the lock. *Suka sin.* How had she learned to do that?

Ana had her gun up when Bradley, her sister's personal assistant, poked his head around the door. The box he was carrying hit the deck with a squishy sound, and he threw his hands in the air.

"Don't shoot!"

Ana rolled her eyes and shoved the Glock semi-automatic into her waistband without thinking, whereupon it immediately slid to mid-thigh.

"Dammit."

"What's 'dammit'?" Tabby asked.

Shit. "It's a bad word, *kotyonak*." Ana had nicknamed her daughter "kitten" when she was a baby because of her quiet cries. "You shouldn't use it, okay? Bradley, what are you doing here?"

"Well, I thought I'd surprise you with a box of cannoli until you tried to kill me."

"If I'd tried to kill you, you'd be dead."

"That's not very comforting." It wasn't meant to be. "Why are you all white?"

"Mama drop the cocaine," Tabby told him, one arm around the dog.

Ana's heart lurched. On the surface, Tabby had recovered well from her unplanned vacation with a Colombian drug producer, but every so often, there'd be a little reminder of a time Ana would rather forget. Would they ever erase the memories? She wiped some of the flour off Tabby's face with her thumbs, but her dark brown hair was still full of it. They both needed a shower.

"It's not cocaine, kitten. It's flour."

"Flowers have petals."

Bradley crouched down beside Tabby as Ana rummaged around in her pants to retrieve the gun.

"It's a special kind of flower, chicky. Do you like flowers?"

"Yes. And Iri likes them."

Sort of. Iriska, Ana and Sam's rescued pit bull, liked to shit on flowers, which wasn't quite the same thing. Ana crouched down too, putting herself at her daughter's eye level.

"Tabby, you mustn't climb on Iri to open the door. It's not safe." They'd have to get an extra bolt to put right at the top of the door or something. In many ways, life had been much easier when they'd both resided in a prison cell. "Do you understand?"

"But I like Bradley."

"It might not always be Bradley. Please, promise me you won't open the door again."

"But you open it."

"That's different."

"Why?"

Give me strength. Ana loved her daughter more than anything, but the fact that Tabby had inherited her curiosity as well as Sam's stubbornness sometimes left her exasperated. Parenting was hard, especially having to work things out as she went along. Short of holding a seance, she couldn't ask for guidance from her own mother, and her father was rotting in the ground too. Not that she'd ever have wanted to ask *him* for advice.

"If you open the door, I jump and drop the cannoli," Bradley said. "You like cannoli, don't you?"

Tabby nodded solemnly, and Ana threw a silent

thank you in Bradley's direction. Then shook her head, trying to dislodge the stupid. Why was she thanking him for sneaking into her apartment building?

"Bradley, why didn't you use the intercom?"

Footsteps sounded in the hallway, soft, almost inaudible, but Ana didn't draw her gun again. She may have only met her half-sister a short time ago, but she already knew the way Emmy moved.

"Bradley, what the fuck are you doing up here? I told you to wait outside. The gate to your parking garage is stuck," Emmy added for Ana's benefit. "The repair guy's working on it, but I had to park on the street and Bradley didn't want to walk because his shoes are pinching."

"A cute guy held the door open for me, and I figured it'd be easier to come right up."

"*Never* come right up," Emmy and Ana said in unison.

As usual, Bradley sidestepped the issue completely. "What really happened in here? Tabby's right—it looks like Eduardo's having a party."

Eduardo was another Colombian, higher up the food chain than the *mudak* who'd held Tabby captive, and one of two men Emmy had adopted as a sort of pseudo-father. Which made him Ana's father too. If a year ago, someone had told her she'd spend time with a drug lord without plotting his murder, she'd have laughed them right out of Russia. Or at least, she would've done if she'd ever laughed. It was only since she left the mother country that she'd felt a little of the burden lift, the burden she'd shouldered her entire life.

Now? Now she had other people to help with the load.

Which meant she could be a stay-at-home mom and set cakes instead of crooked politicians on fire.

"I dropped a bag of flour."

"You *dropped* a bag of flour?" Emmy asked. Her unspoken words? *You never used to make mistakes like that.* "And why does the apartment smell of burnt sugar?"

"The dog distracted me, and I stumbled, and I forgot to turn the stove down, and...yes, I made a mistake, okay?" Ana tossed the Glock on the coffee table and slumped onto the sofa, then groaned when she remembered she was covered in flour. "I just want to be a regular mom with a regular kid. Why is it all so hard?"

"Don't look at me. I don't do the children thing."

"Regular mom?" Bradley scoffed. "You're standing here in gloom because the drapes are closed in the middle of the day, your daughter can name all the parts of a gun but has no idea what a Flower Power doll is, and she's dressed like she's going to a funeral."

Snipers were a very real threat, okay? Ana and Sam were building a new house near Emmy's and that would have bulletproof glass in every window, but until it was ready for them to move into, they were staying in what had once been Sam's bachelor pad. Hence the closed curtains. It was a perfectly sensible precaution.

Ana put her hands on her hips, and Bradley gulped and took a step back. Why did she make everyone so nervous? She didn't mean to. Okay, so there was a second pistol hidden behind the sofa cushion, complete with a suppressor, but she wouldn't actually shoot him with it. Neither would Tabby by accident—the .22 had been custom-built by Emmy's colleague Nate, and the fingerprint scanner in the trigger meant only selected people could fire it.

"The pistol's for self-defence. And black's practical —you told me that last week."

"Self-defence?" He rolled his eyes. "Puh-lease. And when I said black was practical, I was talking about evening wear. How many three-year-old ninjas do you see at preschool?"

"Fine, I'll get her different clothes."

"It's not just the clothes, doll. If you don't want her to get picked on for being a freak, then we need to teach her to act like an all-American preschooler."

"Tabby's not a freak." How fucking dare he? Ana's voice had turned quiet. Deathly quiet. The softness scared people more than raising the volume—the man who trained her had taught her that—and Bradley edged towards the door. "She's *not*."

"She can name more terrorist organisations than she can cartoon characters," Emmy pointed out.

"What are you saying?"

"I'm saying Bradley's right. Just this once," she added hastily. "And don't ask me to repeat that."

Ana sagged back against the cushions again, the gun a hard lump against one butt cheek. Deep down, she'd known Tabby didn't quite fit in with her peers, but how could she change that? Ana didn't know anything about cartoon characters either.

"What should I do?" she whispered. Assassinating a president was far easier than trying to assimilate into suburban Virginia. Ana should know—she'd managed the former twice and was now failing spectacularly at the latter. Sam found their new life easier to cope with, but he went out to work most days.

Emmy shrugged. "Sign up for cable?"

"You don't have cable?" Bradley gasped.

"Who knows? I never watch TV. You think I should?"

"Yes, and I also think you should go out and do normal girl stuff."

"Like what?"

"Like shopping."

Emmy narrowed her eyes. "There's more to life than shopping, Bradley."

"Then what about joining a fitness class?"

"I'm already fit," Ana told him.

"Then pretend you're not, duh."

"That's just a waste of time."

"No, it's called socialising." Bradley grimaced. "On second thought, let's forget that. How about finding a different hobby?"

"Such as?"

"Scrapbooking? Knitting? Baking?" He glanced towards the kitchen. "Perhaps not baking either."

"I can knit already."

"You can?" Emmy sounded surprised.

"*Da*, a crime syndicate was laundering money through a yarn store in Moscow, and I had to infiltrate it." Ana had strangled the ringleader with the yarn then left him sitting in the back room, a note pinned to his eyeball with a knitting needle that she'd jammed all the way into his temporal lobe. That was long before she had Tabby, but she still remembered how to knit a fucking scarf. "I can't see the benefits of scrapbooking."

Hard to paper-cut someone to death, although Ana was willing to try it.

No.

No!

Death by a thousand cuts wasn't compatible with retirement, and she'd always sworn that if she escaped Russia, that was it. Bye-bye Seven, world-class assassin, also known as Lilith and a thousand other names, and hello Anastasia—model girlfriend, amicable neighbour, and doting mother of Tabitha Quinn.

"Actually, maybe I *should* give the scrapbooking a try," she said after a moment.

"Have you lost your fucking mind?" Emmy asked. "What're you gonna do? Stab someone with the scissors?"

Scissors? Of course. Keep the blades nice and sharp, and—

Fuck.

"No. No stabbing and no scissors. I'll try the shopping."

Bradley's eyes lit up. "Fandabidozi! And you're in luck—Emmy's next job just got rescheduled, which means we can all go and buy stuff together this weekend."

"You know what?" Emmy said. "Ana might've quit the game, but I still kill people. No way am I giving up a weekend of R & R to traipse around the shops."

"Ana's your sister. You should be supportive."

"Sure, I'll be supportive. I'll vacuum her apartment. I'll scrub the burnt bits off the stove. Hell, I'll even wash the flour off the damn dog. But unless it sells guns, I'm not going near a store, and I'm especially not going near a store with you."

CHAPTER 2

"OOH, IT FITS perfectly. Now, should we get the sunshine or the grape?" Bradley muttered half to himself as Ana stared at her reflection in the changing-room mirror. The yellow shift dress *did* fit like a second skin, but somebody else's skin. A skin fucking suit. She shuddered, and Emmy gave her a strange look.

"What?" Ana asked.

"Isn't that my line?"

"This dress doesn't work for me."

"Nonsense," Bradley said, fussing with Ana's hair. She wanted to slap his hand away, but a regular girl would be grateful for the attention, wouldn't she? "Hmm, the grape matches your eyes, whereas the sunshine clashes with your attitude. Would it kill you to smile? Anyone would think you were being tortured."

In Russia, Ana had spent years dreaming of escape, but this...this felt more like a nightmare. The changing room was full of squealing women and harried assistants carrying armfuls of clothes, towers of shoeboxes, and an Aladdin's Cave of accessories. The women were in various states of undress, but nobody objected to Bradley's presence. In fact, several had asked him for style tips.

Emmy had tried to veto the trip to New York. She'd begged, she'd pleaded, she'd explained that she had to travel to Eastern Europe to hunt down a genocidal politician, but Bradley called her on her lie and insisted they were coming to the Big Apple. Why hadn't Emmy just refused to go? Because Bradley had threatened to redecorate her living room if they stayed in Virginia, and Ana had seen the book of fabric swatches in his hand. Orange. They were all orange, from a muted peach to glaring neon.

Then Mrs. Fairfax, Emmy's housekeeper, had served up pumpkin soup for lunch, and no way was that a coincidence. Bradley played dirty. The soup was followed by butternut squash risotto with sweet potato fries for dinner, and when Mrs. Fairfax brought out a fruit salad of mango, cantaloupe, and papaya for breakfast, Emmy had caved.

"Fine. We'll go to New York. For two days. That's it."

"Nice try. Sloane says your schedule's empty for four."

Sloane was Emmy's assistant, and a model of efficiency. Ana snorted as she poured her glass of orange juice, which with hindsight was a mistake because it attracted Bradley's attention.

"I don't know why you're laughing. You don't even have a schedule."

Now it was Emmy's turn to snigger.

"*Zhizn' ebet meya,*" Ana muttered.

"Nah, sis, life is fucking *us.*"

And that was how they ended up in their current situation.

When Ana used to lie awake at night, hoping for a normal life, she'd envisioned something much quieter. Days spent working as a waitress or a cleaner or a supermarket cashier while Tabby was at school, and in the evenings, quality time at home with her daughter. Quality time that didn't involve chiffon, sparkles, or feathers.

But there they were in New York with all that and more. Sam had escaped to the other side of the world, Iriska was staying with the groom who looked after Emmy's devil of a horse, and Bradley had whisked Ana, Emmy and Tabby off to an expensive version of hell. Life hadn't turned out quite the way Ana thought. But since Tabby seemed happy, swinging her legs as she sat on a low leather stool in her princess dress, Ana would put up with the shopping. She attempted a smile. Did that work? It wasn't something she'd had much practice at.

"How about we get neither dress?" Emmy suggested. "They're not really Ana's style."

Bradley put his hands on his hips. "But they both look fabulous."

"I can't run in this," Ana said.

"Well, of course not. You're not supposed to run at PTA meetings."

"PTA meetings?"

"I thought you wanted to become an all-American mom? They go to PTA meetings."

Nowhere in Ana's daydreams had PTA meetings come up. The thought of spending hours having to be nice to other moms while they discussed banalities filled her with a cold dread. Freedom was better than what had come before, but it was also hard. Much harder than she'd imagined. A week ago, Ana had overheard Emmy speaking with her husband, Black, and he'd mentioned the word "institutionalised."

At first, she'd been angry. What gave him the right to judge her like that? But the more she thought about it, the more she realised he was right. She'd spent her whole life as the slave of a Russian madman, and slotting into a new world wasn't as easy as she'd hoped. Sure, she'd been shopping on undercover jobs, but it was just an act. The mission had always been front and centre of her mind. The last time she visited a department store like this one, she'd been posing as an oligarch's girlfriend, and as she giggled and smiled and agreed with his opinions while she tried on clothes, she'd been quietly plotting to kill him.

Perhaps if she distracted herself by planning a murder, time would pass quicker?

But who to murder? Hmm...

"Earth to Ana?" Bradley waved a hand in front of her eyes.

"Huh?" Oh, right. The dress. She crouched down as best she could considering the restrictions of the outfit. "Tabby, which colour do you like best?"

"Black."

"Out of yellow and purple."

Tabby thought for a moment, chewing her bottom lip. Sometimes, Ana couldn't believe she'd played a part in creating something that cute.

"Purple."

"Then it's settled. The purple one."

Bradley clapped his hands together. "Excellent. Now we just need to find shoes and accessories to match. And don't groan—this is fun."

"No, it isn't," Emmy said.

"Stop being such a sourpuss and try your dresses on. Anyone would think you'd rather be at work."

"I would."

"Dresses. Now."

Strange how Emmy stood up to criminals and despots, everyone from street thugs to the man who'd ruled Ana's life, yet she accepted orders from a small man with turquoise-and-pink hair. And not only that, she paid him money to boss her around.

"Try these pumps on." Bradley set a pair of shiny green shoes with four-inch heels in front of Ana. "And don't tell me they're too high because they aren't."

Ana had a foot halfway into the first shoe before realisation dawned. Bradley bossed *her* around too. And she let him.

Dammit.

"Pick anything you want, chicky. How about a Flower Power doll? Or a Bake 'n' Serve stove? Or a My Little Pony?"

Tabby's eyes widened as she took in the scene before her. They'd left the sixteen bags of clothes he'd purchased with the concierge and taken the elevator up one floor to the toy department, a rainbow of colour where things sparkled and shone and made strange noises. Back in Russia, Tabby had only owned one toy, a cuddly rabbit named Twixy who'd gotten lost in the madness when they first came to the US. Part of Ana wanted to buy her the world, but she also didn't want to spoil her daughter.

"Anything?" Tabby asked.

"Anything," Bradley confirmed. "Or everything. If you ask your Aunt Emmy nicely, I'm sure she'll buy you a toy store."

"No toy store," Emmy and Ana said together, but Tabby was already running towards the nearest shelf. Ana hurried to follow. She'd nearly lost her daughter once, and now she hated to let the little girl out of her sight. Even the thought of Tabby going to preschool terrified her, but she couldn't keep her daughter hidden away for her entire life. Being held prisoner for the first two and a half years had been bad enough.

Where did Tabby head? To the dolls? To the plush animals? To the craft section? No. Ana caught up with her in the boys' section, where she was trying to shove a toy gun into her waistband. The trigger guard got caught on the pink belt Bradley had bought for her, but she quickly forgot about that as she picked up a plastic sword and began waving it around. Ana grabbed it just before she whacked a bigger boy in the face.

"Tabby, you mustn't do that."

"But I want to be like you, Mama."

Oh, fuck. Ana didn't know whether to be proud or horrified. Yes, Tabitha was smart, but three-year-old girls were supposed to play dress-up and colour shit in, not stage mock-assassinations. Upon reflection, horror was the appropriate reaction.

"She's a chip off the block, isn't she?" Emmy said.

Bradley appeared behind her, clutching a purple teddy bear. "Heaven help us all."

"What am I meant to do?" Ana whispered.

"Uh..."

Bradley knelt beside Tabby and gently uncurled her fingers from a half-size version of Thor's hammer, the head thankfully made from foam rather than some Asgardian metal.

"You shouldn't hit people, chicky."

"But Mama—"

"Only hits bad guys. Do you know how to tell the bad guys from the good guys?"

Tabby shook her head.

"The bad guys wear handcuffs. So you only hit people who are wearing handcuffs, okay?"

"Okay." Phew. Crisis averted. "Is Daddy a bad guy?"

Fuck.

"Why would you say that?" Bradley asked.

"Mama handcuffed him to the bed."

Emmy burst out laughing, and Ana's cheeks burned. Shit, shit, shit. She thought she'd heard footsteps in the hallway outside the bedroom door the other night, but when she'd shushed Sam to listen, there was only silence. Ana had checked on her daughter after they'd finished, but Tabby had been sleeping peacefully. How much had she seen?

"Uh, what were you doing up?"

"I wanted water. I come to ask, but Iri helped me."

Presumably, she'd stood on the dog to reach the tap. That damn mutt was too patient for its own good.

"Your daddy isn't a bad guy," Bradley told her, his voice skipping as he tried to swallow down his chuckles.

"Then why—"

Ana snatched a toy crossbow from the nearest shelf. "Why don't we buy this? We can get two and have a contest."

Tabby's face lit up. "Yes! And I want clever clothes."

"What?"

Clever clothes? What was she talking about? Sure, Ana had heard of the Internet of Things and self-driving vehicles, but clever clothes?

"Clever clothes. Auntie Dan likes clever clothes."

"Leather?" Emmy asked. "Do you mean leather clothes?"

Tabby's brow creased as she puzzled over the question, and she looked so sweet Ana wanted to take a picture. But she only held the expression for a second.

"Maybe leather. Can I have leather?"

"I'm sure we can get you a leather outfit. Right, Bradley?"

"Do I get any say in this?" Ana asked.

"Sure. Feel free to explain to your daughter why she can't dress like a rock chick."

"Uh, Tabby..."

But Tabby didn't listen. She was too busy trying to stuff a sucker dart into the crossbow. Ana took both away before she shot someone's eye out.

"Later."

"Now! I need to shoot the sky."

"Why?"

"To get stars."

Obviously. "Why do you want stars?"

"Because I'm a ninja, and ninjas need stars. To throw."

"Who told you that?"

"Daddy."

Good thing Sam had gone to England for a week because Ana might have been forced to kill him otherwise.

"You mustn't shoot things, *kotyonak*. Or throw them."

"But—"

Bradley knelt beside her. "The stars only come out

at night."

"Tonight we shoot stars?"

"No, chicky," Bradley said. "But I've got a fantabulous surprise for everyone later. You're gonna love it."

A surprise? The words were enough to strike fear into the heart of even the most hardened warrior. Ana glanced at Emmy, but a small shake of the head said her sister didn't know any more than she did.

"What surprise?" Ana asked.

"Duh. If I told you, it wouldn't be a surprise, would it?"

"I hate surprises."

"This one's amazing."

"Does it involve music, dancing, or glitter?" Emmy asked.

"Maybe a tiny bit."

"Then we're not going. All we want is a quiet night in."

"But I've already arranged everything."

"Then un-arrange it."

"What was that?" Bradley picked Tabby up and carried her towards a display of cartoon-themed accessories. "I can't hear you."

"Fuck," Emmy muttered under her breath. "Next time he tries this shit, I'm gonna buy a pair of sunglasses, and then he can paint my living room whatever colour he wants."

CHAPTER 3

THE STREETS OF London are paved with gold,
The mountains of Alaska sparkle in the cold.
Spain and Egypt gleam in the sun,
But for magic and glitter, there's only one
Alvenna!

Bradley sang along with the show tunes, whooping and cheering as a bunch of actors ran through the aisles, tossing sparkly confetti everywhere. Emmy cursed under her breath while Ana covered Tabby's eyes with her hands. At least if she was shielding her daughter, she couldn't get tempted to drown one of the oh-so-perky performers in a bucket of fucking glitter. Another handful of sparkles covered her, and she forced herself to take a deep breath.

This is their job. They're paid to make people's lives a misery, just like I was.

Emmy gripped Ana's arm. "Don't kill Bradley. At least, not here in the theatre. Getting rid of the body could be tricky."

"I have glitter in my fucking bra."

"Look on the bright side—at least Tabby's not wearing black."

No, she was wearing every colour imaginable, topped off with strings of Mardi Gras beads and a bloody tiara. Next time, Ana would personally school her daughter in the art of Ninjitsu while Bradley went to the musical alone.

According to the program, *Glitter: The Musical* was a heartwarming tale of a young girl who travelled to New York seeking fame and fortune, only to fall through a portal to another realm after a mysterious goblin spiked her drink. In any other world, that would be grounds for a lawsuit, but instead of running screaming to the nearest police station, Maisie Martins had rented an apartment and made herself at home in Alvenna. Her roommates were a unicorn and a flamingo.

Apparently, Bradley's friend Ishmael had designed the costumes, which was how they'd ended up with front-row tickets for the matinee performance. Ana hadn't met Ishmael yet, but she suspected he ate magic mushrooms for breakfast and LSD for lunch, sprinkled with peyote and washed down with Red Bull. And speaking of magic mushrooms, fuck only knew where Bradley planned to drag them for dinner.

Around them, the audience danced in their seats as they sang with the performers. How did all these people know the words? Did they come printed on the back of their tickets to purgatory? At least Tabby seemed to be enjoying herself as Bradley encouraged her to clap and wave her arms in the air. Specks of glitter flew off their hands and landed everywhere—the seats, the floor, the people behind them, the screen of Emmy's tablet.

"What are you doing?" Ana asked her.

"Catching up on my emails. Might as well do something useful."

Except Bradley snatched the tablet out of her hands. "No work! Can't you just act normal for once?"

"How is this normal? The entire audience is on acid."

"Shut up and sing."

"You realise the two are mutually exclusive, right?"

"Blah, blah, blah. Quit being so boring."

Bradley lifted Tabby onto his lap, and she giggled. *Giggled*. Ana might have hated the show, but she couldn't be totally pissed off, not when her daughter was happy. In Russia, Tabby had never laughed, not once. She'd barely even smiled, despite Ana's efforts to shield her from the worst of the shit General Zacharov had thrown in their direction.

But Ana still wasn't going to sing. No way.

And neither was Emmy, it seemed. Two rainbow-covered crazies gave her dirty looks as she got up to leave.

"Where are you going?" Bradley squeaked. "This is the best bit."

"To the bathroom."

The bathroom? Take letters one, two, and five and you probably got closer to the truth. And who could blame Emmy for that? Ana didn't drink much as a rule, but a shot of vodka to take the edge off the madness seemed like a sensible idea right then. They were only half an hour into a three-hour show, for fuck's sake. And apparently, there was audience participation in the later stages.

"Are you coming?" she asked Ana.

If only. "No, Tabby—"

"Will be fine with Bradley." Emmy leaned in closer. "You have to leave her sometime."

"I do leave her. Last week, I left her with Sam while I went to the gun range."

"Sam's her father. He doesn't count."

Emmy was right. Ana knew she was right, but she still hated to face the truth. Tabby was captivated by the show, bouncing on Bradley's lap in a crowd of hundreds. There were security cameras at every exit, including the four fire exits, which were alarmed yet freely accessible should the need to use them arise. Ana had checked. She'd also studied the people around them as they took their seats, and nobody had given off bad vibes. Plus the theatre was opposite a police station, and there was a security guard stationed in the lobby.

Logically, Tabby would be safe if Ana nipped out for a quick drink.

But logic flew out the window when it came to her daughter. In so many ways, Emmy shared Ana's thought processes, feelings, and opinions, but Emmy wasn't a mother. She didn't understand what it felt like to have a child, or worse, the utter terror of losing one.

"Hey! You're blocking the stage," a redhead in the row behind complained. "Either sit down or leave, would you?"

Don't murder the suka *in the tutu, Ana.*

She made herself un-ball her fists and focus on the future instead. How would she ever walk away on that first day of preschool if she didn't start practising now? She had to do it, didn't she? Otherwise she'd spend Tabby's early years camped out in the school parking lot with a gun.

"One drink, *da*?"

"Sure," Emmy said. "One drink."

A few other desperate souls had already taken up residence in the bar off the lobby. Mostly men. The majority of them twinkled under the lights—chandeliers, of course, because having a simple strip light or two would probably be a crime in a place like that—and a trail of confetti led back the way they'd come. The barstools were upholstered in silver fabric, the bar top was made out of clear resin filled with glitter, and each table came with a unicorn snow globe. A TV in the corner live-streamed the stage, but thankfully somebody had put it on mute. Even better, the camera looked as if it was attached to the front of the mezzanine balcony, and the angle meant Ana could see the silhouettes of the people seated in the first two rows. Including Bradley and Tabby.

A little of the tension left her.

"Can I get you a drink?" the barman asked. His accent was British, something northern by the sound of it, not London with a hint of fake posh like Emmy's. Ana was making the effort to speak with a US accent in New York, and slowly, slowly, it became easier.

"Vodka and orange juice."

Potatoes and fruit. That was healthy, right? And if she stuck to vodka, she wouldn't smell like an alcoholic in front of her daughter. Emmy followed the theme, sticking to the drink of her motherland.

"Gin and tonic for me. Hendricks, cucumber, easy on the ice." She dropped a fifty-dollar bill on the bar. "Keep the change."

"Thanks, sweetheart. I'll make them doubles." The barman cut his eyes towards the TV. "Anyone here to see that palaver needs all the help they can get."

They settled in a quiet corner with their drinks, out

of earshot of the other patrons but still in view of the screen. Ana's quick glances didn't go unnoticed.

"She'll be okay, you know," Emmy said.

"*Da.*" Ana kept telling herself that.

"Blackwood has the security contract for the theatre. I stuck an extra guy on the schedule tonight, and since he saw me walk through the lobby, he'll be pretty fucking alert. Does that help?"

"I guess. He's good?"

Emmy nodded. "He wants a spot on my Special Projects team."

"Will he get one?"

"The jury's still out on that, but he's certainly more competent than your average security guard. Enjoy your drink and stop worrying all the time."

"It's normal to worry." At least, Ana assumed as much. "Isn't it?"

"Yes, but it's also normal to leave your kid with a babysitter."

"I'm still learning about this stuff, okay? I mean, I did a lot of undercover work, but living like a regular person without backup is so much harder than I thought it'd be."

"You've got backup, honey."

"I know. Fuck, I know, and I still pinch myself every morning." Ana caught Emmy's quiet snort. "You think I'm kidding?" She rolled up a sleeve to reveal a purple mark on her forearm, two fingernail-marks clear to see. Her freedom-in-America bruise. "Sam thinks I'm crazy."

"You are."

"Fuck you too. And that wasn't what I meant."

"Then what?"

"It's not just the practicalities. In Russia, people did all the day-to-day chores for me, yes. I never had to buy clothes or go to the grocery store or hire a plumber or iron shirts or take the dog to get its damn shots, but I always longed to do those things because then I'd be normal."

"And now you *are* doing those things."

"*Da.*"

"But you're not enjoying it?"

"*Nyet.*" Ana shook her head, finally admitting what she'd been trying to deny for the last few weeks. She was living her dream, but she was also bored out of her mind. "Even though this was what I always wanted," she murmured, almost to herself.

"What *you* wanted? Or what you thought you should want for Tabby?"

Damn.

Emmy was right, wasn't she? She'd hit the nail on its painful little head. Ana had yearned to escape from Russia for a long time, but her dreams of suburbia had only started after her daughter was born. She'd desperately wanted Tabby to grow up safe in an environment that didn't include regular gunfire or marching drills, but she'd never considered the alternatives—musicals and bouncy castles and the KinderSong Club. She'd signed Tabby up for six weeks of KinderSong after a woman she met in the elevator of her apartment building recommended it, and it'd been a disaster. Not only had the Kinder Leader expected Ana to sing too, but he'd also looked at Tabby funny, which gave Ana the creeps. She'd borrowed his phone and forwarded the contents to Emmy, and he'd been arrested two days later. At least Ana had gotten a refund on the other five sessions.

"I guess maybe this was what I wanted for Tabby."

"But you need to be happy too. Why don't you hire an assistant?"

"A Bradley? No."

"A housekeeper, then?"

"I imagine watching somebody else clean my apartment is even duller than doing it myself. And how can I justify employing someone when I'm home all day at the moment? It's not just the chores that frustrate me. It's having no purpose." Ana gestured towards the TV, where Maisie Martins was dancing with the unicorn. "Regular people really like that shit? Is this what they do with their lives? Go shopping and sing badly?"

"I guess it depends on how you define 'regular.'" Emmy took a long swallow of her gin and tonic. "And I'm pretty sure that doesn't include us."

Right. Ana knocked back the rest of her vodka and motioned at the barman to bring another drink for them both. One more, and then she'd stop. Even pre-Tabby, she'd rarely gotten drunk. The last time, she'd been eighteen, and General Zacharov had made her swim as a punishment, one minute of front crawl for every minute she'd spent in the bar. Nothing like being thrown into the freezing waters of Lake Baikal to sober you up in a hurry. She'd gone down with hypothermia, but the general had just snapped that it was an occupational hazard and told her to toughen up.

A sick, sick part of Ana missed her old life. Not the general and his volatile personality, but the challenge of facing death and punching it in the damn face. Of not only dodging the Grim Reaper, but hacking his head off with his fucking scythe and laughing while she did it.

But she'd never tell anyone that, not even Emmy. They'd have her committed.

"No, we're the antithesis of regular."

"If you're bored, I can find you something to do. Your desk at Blackwood's still empty."

Ana hadn't set foot in the office since her desperate search for Tabby had ended. When she got her daughter back, she'd thought that part of her life was over. Done. But Emmy's offer was tempting, more tempting than it should have been. What would Sam say if Ana announced she wanted to resurrect her old career?

"I quit all that."

Why, even to Ana's own ears, did those words sound unconvincing?

"I'm not suggesting you pick up where you left off. How about mission planning? Or research?"

"A desk job?"

"Perhaps you could help out with training? That'd be more hands-on."

True, but playing nicely with others had never been Ana's strong point.

"I'll think about it."

She did think about it, all the way through their second drink and the packets of potato chips Emmy insisted on eating, but by the time she drained her glass, she was still none the wiser. The thought of going back to work left her with an unfamiliar feeling of apprehension, not so much because of the job itself but more from the prospect of having to integrate with new people. But could she really spend the rest of her life pretending to love retirement?

She very much suspected the answer was no.

"Another drink?" Emmy asked.

"We should get back." Tabby didn't seem to be missing Ana, but Ana was missing Tabby.

"Fine, but I need to find some Tylenol first. The music's giving me a headache."

"Doesn't Bradley have any?"

"Nope. He's got organic ginseng and goji berry capsules."

The barman leaned in to pick up the empty glasses. "The vending machine in the ladies' bathroom sells Tylenol. We have to refill it twice a week."

"Cheers."

As Emmy pushed open the bathroom door, she looked back at Ana. "Ready for hell, part two? Maisie Martins and her flamingo are waiting."

"I'm always ready."

And Ana needed to be, because hell turned out to be closer than either of them thought.

CHAPTER 4

"DO YOU SMELL that?" Ana asked.

"Smell what? I reek of that sodding perfume Bradley doused me with."

He'd tried to spray Ana too, but she'd grabbed the bottle and tossed it out of the bedroom window. He should've held onto it tighter if he was gonna try that trick. But no matter—top notes of rose and fucking jasmine weren't what Ana smelled.

"Blood." The coppery tang of fresh blood.

Emmy's body tightened almost imperceptibly, and her right hand reached for the gun Ana knew was stashed in her purse.

"Where?" she whispered.

Good question. It only took a second for both of their gazes to lock onto the most likely place—the only closed door in the room. When Ana crouched to look through the three-inch gap under the stall door, she saw a slim pale leg with a pool of blood seeping out from under it. Living or dead? She couldn't tell, but they needed to find out.

"Lift me up?"

Emmy didn't bother to ask for the details, not yet, just clasped her hands together for Ana to step onto, then gave her a boost. Ana's heart sped up as she wriggled over the top of the door, her ass brushing the ceiling.

Was there a threat? The girl was slumped against the wall in front of the toilet, a pair of scissors loosely clasped in her left hand, and no, there was no threat. She didn't move as Ana dropped down beside her, landing softly, and plucked the scissors from her fingers.

Ten more seconds, and Ana had noted the shallow rise of the girl's chest and unlocked the door for Emmy.

"Dead?"

"Alive, but barely."

Blood ran from the girl's wrists onto the grubby tiles, forming a widening puddle and soaking into her jeans. What possessed a woman to attempt suicide in a toilet stall? Ana had contemplated eating a bullet a number of times in her life, but never in a public bathroom. That took a special kind of desperation.

"Let me..." the girl tried, speaking in a soft whisper. "Let...me...die."

No, that wasn't an option.

Once, Ana's own situation had seemed hopeless, but Emmy had fixed it. Now, Ana found herself wanting to pay it forward, to help someone else out of the depths. She pulled off her shirt and used the girl's scissors to hack it into strips as Emmy called nine-one-one. The first priority was to stop the bleeding, and she bound the makeshift bandages around the girl's wrists to staunch the flow. The fabric quickly turned scarlet. After one attempt to pull her arms away, the girl went limp and let Ana get on with it.

The slashes scored across the wrists, while most people serious about suicide cut lengthways instead. Could this be a cry for help rather than a genuine desire to die? Ana didn't believe so, not with the way the girl had locked herself out of sight. Another minute or two, and she'd have bled out anyway. And then there was the weapon. Who tried to kill themselves with scissors? This felt like a panicked, impromptu act by somebody who saw no other choice.

"Ambulance is on its way," Emmy said, then tapped away at her phone again. "Cade? It's Emmy Black. We just found an injured girl in the ladies' bathroom by the bar. When the EMTs arrive, could you show them in here? Thanks." She hung up. "How's it looking?"

"Blood loss is slowing, but she needs fluids."

"Shouldn't be long—the hospital isn't far. I doubt the theatre has more than a basic first aid kit. Do you need more bandages?"

"No, this is okay."

The flow of blood was slowing, and the cotton fabric Ana had wrapped around the girl's wrists would stay in place until she got to the ER. In Russia, Ana had undergone significant medical training, and barring any unforeseen circumstances, the girl should survive. But what about her mental state?

"What's your name?"

The girl gave a barely perceptible shake of her head. A curtain of blonde hair fell over her face, and she stayed silent, her eyes closed.

"Is there anyone we can call? Your parents?"

"No!"

Well, that got a reaction. Was there a problem with her family?

"How about a friend?"

Nothing.

Ana patted the girl down, but her pockets were

empty. No weapons, no phone, no wallet. Why was she even at the theatre? She wasn't covered in glitter like Emmy and Ana, so she hadn't been in the audience for the show.

Emmy unrolled toilet paper and used it to soak up the blood creeping towards the door. The stall was tiny, bordering on claustrophobic, and Ana took a second to organise her thoughts, to block out unwanted emotions and focus on the fundamentals. A reset, General Zacharov had called it. Any time she felt overwhelmed, she was to take a mental step back and concentrate her attention on what was important. With two decades of practice behind her, resetting had become as natural to Ana as breathing.

Emmy pulled off her sweater and gave it to Ana to put on. Just in time, because hurried footsteps sounded in the hallway outside a moment later, together with men's voices.

"In here."

The door crashed open, and a pair of EMTs, one old and one young, took stock of the situation.

"Probable suicide attempt," Emmy told them. "We found her like this when we came to use the bathroom. She's been conscious throughout, but she's lost a lot of blood."

"Has she said anything? Did she give a name?"

"Refused. And family's a no-go too."

"She doesn't have any?"

"Apparently not."

Or at least, not that anybody wanted to discuss with the EMTs.

"Right. Well, we'll do what we can."

"Those cuts are deep. You'll need a vascular

surgeon on standby."

"You have medical training?"

"I'm a nurse back home in England. Here, let me hold that bag of fluids up."

Ana kept out of the way while the EMTs inserted an IV line and added more bandages over the strips of shirt. The cotton was soaked through now, but at least the blood had stopped gushing. A few nosy theatregoers appeared in the doorway, staring, but Cade, Emmy's Special-Projects-wannabe, blocked them with an arm. Ana glared at them too, and they soon moved on. Ghouls.

The girl didn't utter a word as the EMTs strapped her onto a stretcher, but occasionally, she opened her eyes and looked around. What would happen to her? As a suicide risk, she'd probably end up in a psych ward. Either that or they'd toss her out onto the street if they found out she couldn't afford to pay for medical treatment.

Neither seemed like a good prospect.

The medics exited stage left, and Emmy moved to follow.

"Where are you going?" Ana asked.

"To the hospital. Coming?"

"What about Tabby?"

Emmy tapped the Blackwood guy on the shoulder. "Cade, Bradley's still in the auditorium with Ana's daughter. I need you to arrange a car and escort the pair of them to my apartment, then wait with them until we get back, okay?"

"Front row, right?"

"Yup."

"I'll get straight on it."

Oh, that didn't sit well at all. Ana pulled Emmy out of Cade's earshot. "Have a stranger look after Tabby? Are you crazy?"

"Bradley's not a stranger."

"Cade is."

"Not to me. Look, I get that it's difficult, but you have to loosen your grip a little. Besides..." She nodded in the direction the EMTs had taken. "Aren't you curious?"

Yes, Ana was, and more than that, she felt desperately sorry for the blonde girl. If there was anything they could do to help, they needed to try. Ana had walked by far too many times in the past, acting on the orders of a man who had no heart, and now she wanted to change.

"Okay, let's go. But Cade needs to call us before they leave the theatre and check in as soon as they reach the apartment."

"I'll have Bradley live-stream the trip to your phone, how about that?"

Ana was about to agree when she realised just how ridiculous that sounded. "The phone calls will be fine."

CHAPTER 5

THE BLONDE WENT straight into surgery, and Ana spent an hour pacing the hospital corridor, not so much from worry over the girl's health as with annoyance because the wait meant she could have taken Tabby back to Emmy's apartment herself. The hospital receptionist wouldn't give them any details, anyway. Something about not being relatives.

"Why hasn't Cade called? What if we were wrong and it wasn't a suicide attempt? There could be a psycho roaming around the theatre, and Tabby's—"

"Relax, honey." Emmy sat on a gurney, swinging her legs. "They just haven't left yet."

"How do you know that?"

"Because I know Bradley. If Ishmael designed the costumes, you can bet Bradley's wangled backstage access, and there's no way he'd pass up the opportunity to get bedazzled up close and personal."

"What if—"

Emmy's phone rang, Maisie Martins belting out one of the tracks from the show, and Ana recognised it as the ringtone Bradley had set for himself. He'd tried to do the same with Ana's phone, but she'd picked him up, carried him out of the room, and told him his next stop would be the swimming pool if he attempted that trick again.

Why had Bradley called Emmy and not her? Was something wrong?

"Is everything okay?" she asked, crowding in close.

"Take a chill pill, doll. We haven't even left yet."

"Told you," Emmy mouthed.

"But the show finished ages ago."

"Yes, and then Maisie herself gave Tabby a tour of the theatre. I have the cutest picture of her in a kitten costume, and they sang together on stage. I'll send the video right over."

Thank fuck for that. Not for the video, but the fact that Tabby was okay.

"So you're leaving now?"

"Not yet. Tabby still has to get her hair and make-up done again."

"Hair and make-up?" *Again?* "She's not even three years old."

"And it's never too early to start. You don't want her to reach her teens and still not know how to do winged eyeliner, do you?"

"Actually—"

"Cade told me you went to the hospital with a girl you found in the bathroom?"

"We did, but about the make-up..."

"So we asked around, and we're almost totally certain we know who she is."

Cade's voice sounded in the background. "Can I borrow the—"

"Shush, I'm speaking. Is it true? She cut her wrists?"

"Bradley, who is she?" Emmy asked, her tone a cross between impatient and exasperated.

"Did she?"

"Yes, but—"

"Wow, that's so sad. We should definitely send flowers. Tulips. Her purse has tulips on—so pretty—and there's a florist on Lexington Avenue that does the most fantabulous bouquets."

"Her name, Bradley. Tell me her name before I have to shake it out of you."

"Oh, it's Jennifer Fleming. She's a make-up artist here at the theatre. Apparently, those super-duper jewelled eyelashes were her idea, and not everyone can create a style so dramatic yet so natural. Thank goodness you saved her."

"How do you know?"

"Because I tried it on Dan once, and she looked like a drag queen."

"I meant, how do you know it's her?"

Finally, Cade managed to wrestle the phone away from Bradley. "We asked around about a missing blonde, and one of the pixies told us Jennifer got a message on her phone in the first half of the show, said she needed a moment, then never came back. The others had to cover for her, and they weren't happy about it."

"We need to find a picture of her."

"Already done. Most of the crew here are friends with her on Facebook. I'll send the link over, but I recognised her from the photos."

"Good work."

"One of the costume people also said she'd had issues back home."

"What kind of problems? Where's home?"

"Some Podunk town in Oklahoma. She lost her mom, and there may have been other family stuff too."

"Any idea what?"

"Sorry. By all accounts, she doesn't like to talk about her personal life much."

"Okay, thanks. Now, get Tabby home safely, and don't let Bradley near anything else shiny."

"The first I can do, but the second..."

"Just try, yeah?"

Emmy's phone buzzed almost instantly with an incoming message, and she signed into Facebook. Not with her own name, obviously—now she was Ellery La Zulema, a thirty-year-old PA with a love of cats and a habit of posting pictures of her dinner.

"La Zulema?" Ana asked. "Where's that from?"

"Argentina, I believe. It's a kind of wine. I suspect Mack set up this profile while she was drinking it." Emmy scrolled down further, past a picture of Ellery's new shoes—lime-green pumps with spike heels—and a whole collection of alcohol-related memes. "Yup, definitely drinking."

Jennifer's profile painted a very different picture to Ellery's. She appeared to be fond of baby animals, houseplants, and inspirational quotes. Occasionally, she'd comment on make-up-related posts, usually offering advice or encouragement, but she didn't come across as a busybody, more as a mentor. And she seemed happy, although Ana knew that even the most cheerful of people could suffer from depression.

"What happened to you, Jennifer?" Emmy muttered.

It was a question that only one person could answer.

And it seemed that Emmy intended to ask her the question.

Right after shift change, she sauntered out of the hospital through a side door, rubbed her eyes to make them red and smudged her mascara a bit, turned her face up so the rain dampened it, and then burst back in through the front door with Ana at her heels.

"My sister," she blurted at the receptionist, her accent now American with a slight twang. "I heard my sister was brought here."

"What's her name, ma'am?"

"Jennifer. Jennifer Fleming. The people at the theatre said she was hurt, and— Oh my gosh, is she going to be okay?"

"She's not on the system. Are you sure she's here?"

"I-I-I think she was unconscious. With..." Emmy gripped her right wrist with her left hand. "With... Why would she do that? Why?"

"That sounds like our Jane Doe. You're her sister, you say?"

"Older sister. I should have been there for her more, but I've been having some problems at work, and — Do you know how she is?"

The receptionist gave an encouraging smile, but her eyes were tired. "She's just gotten out of surgery."

"Can I see her?"

"I'll have someone take you through." She peered at Ana over the top of her glasses. "Are you family too?"

"Her cousin."

"Of course." The receptionist's gaze switched back to Emmy. "I see the resemblance."

CHAPTER 6

AN HOUR LATER, Ana and Emmy sat beside Jennifer's bed as her eyes flickered open. Emmy had arranged for her to have a private room, so at least they could have a conversation without the Friday night party crowd listening in.

Even better, Cade had called to say that he, Bradley, and Tabby were safely ensconced in Emmy's apartment. Bradley had sent a video of Tabby on stage at the theatre, and her hair was pink. Neon fucking pink. Perhaps it was best that Ana stayed at the hospital for a while after all, because if she went home right away, she might get tempted to send Bradley to the emergency room instead.

"Hey," Emmy said as Jennifer rejoined the land of the living. "Welcome back."

Jennifer closed her eyes and groaned.

"That bad?"

"I messed up *again*." The words came out as a whisper. "It was you at the theatre?"

"Yes."

"You should've left me there."

"Nah, the blood was making a mess of the floor."

Jennifer's eyes popped open once more, most likely in shock at Emmy's macabre sense of humour.

"I'm so sorry. I didn't think..."

Her voice was high-pitched, almost musical, and definitely out of place in New York. Fucking hell, the fact she was apologising for being so close to despair that she'd tried to kill herself said a lot about Jennifer's character. She was as sweet as the fluffy bunnies on her Facebook page.

"Don't be sorry for that. What can we do to help?"

"Nothing."

"There's always something. If you want to speak to someone—someone professional, I mean—I can arrange that."

"You mean like a psychiatrist?"

Emmy nodded. "A therapist. Doesn't everyone have a therapist nowadays?"

"I'm not crazy. I'm not. I... I'm... I just..."

"Couldn't see another way out?"

"Yes, exactly."

"Way out of what?"

Silence. Jennifer made a show of studying the bandages on her wrists, now thick white instead of the makeshift floral Ana had used earlier. And don't even get Ana started on the "floral" part.

"We might be able to lend a hand. A problem shared and all that."

"I can't share. He... He... I just can't."

Who was *he*?

"Was it the message you got?" Ana asked. "On your phone?"

Jennifer stiffened, and the tiny bit of colour in her cheeks faded to a deathly white. A yes, then. Where was the phone now? At the theatre? Did Bradley have any idea?

"An ex-boyfriend?" Emmy guessed.

"Not a boyfriend."

"A stalker? A pervert? An overbearing boss?"

"He said if I told anyone, he'd..." She shook her head. "I can't say."

"He's blackmailing you? Because the police can help with that."

"No! No police."

"Well, unless you want to have another go with the scissors, I'm not sure doing nothing's an option."

Fuck, that was blunt. Even Ana winced inwardly. But Emmy's words shocked Jennifer enough to make her have a rethink on her "don't tell" policy.

"I have to do something," she whispered. "But I don't know what."

"People say I'm good at solving problems. And if it's not something I can fix myself, the chances are I'm acquainted with a person who can. What did this asshole say to you, honey?"

"I met him in a bar two weeks ago. If I was back home in Oklahoma, I'd never have done what I did that night, I swear. But the other girls at the theatre made it sound so normal, and just for once, I wanted to feel like I fit in."

What was bad enough that she'd attempt suicide rather than admit to it?

"You didn't kill anyone, did you?" Ana asked.

"*What*? No way! No, I... I slept with him." Jennifer spoke so softly that Ana had to lean forward to hear. "We had a one-night stand."

That was it? After all the build-up, the revelation was somewhat disappointing. Emmy looked puzzled too.

"People have those every day of the week," she said.

"And from what I hear, they're nothing to write home about most of the time."

"You don't understand. He has pictures. Of me. Of us. And if I don't send him ten thousand dollars by midnight on Sunday, he's going to send them to my friends and family." A tear rolled down her cheek. "My grandpop."

"Are you sure he's not bluffing? If you'd never met him before, how did he get their contact information?"

"He's not bluffing. He sent me some of the pictures and a list of their email addresses as proof. I think he stole the details from my phone while I was asleep. It's locked with my fingerprint, and after we did"—her voice quietened again—"did *it*, I fell asleep. And when I woke up, he was gone. But I'm sure he searched my room because I always fold everything real neat and my drawers were all messy."

Kompromat. Compromising material. In the higher echelons of politics, it made the world go round. At General Zacharov's behest, Ana had been involved in gathering it and using it, and now that he was dead, she'd inherited his secret stash. Well, not inherited it, exactly. After he died, she'd slid the memory cards out of their hiding place in his office while no one was looking and brought them to the US with her. Even Emmy didn't know she had them. Maybe one day they'd come in useful or maybe they wouldn't, but if anyone from the motherland ever made a move against Ana, you'd better believe their secrets were coming out.

But blackmail against an innocent woman? The man deserved to lose body parts.

"I realise that having pictures like that out in the world is embarrassing," Emmy said. "But I guarantee you everyone's seen a naked body before. If you can tough it out for a week or two, it'll blow over."

"Maybe in New York I could do that, but half of the people on that contact list are from my home town. And...and..."

Jennifer sniffled and gulped, trying to hold back her sobs. In Ana's world, tears had been a sign of weakness, and the general didn't tolerate weakness. As a child, Ana had quickly learned not to cry because the punishment was invariably worse than whatever had caused the tears in the first place. It was only when she came to America that her mask had cracked to reveal emotion, and as a consequence of Ana's upbringing, Jennifer's distress left her off balance. Uncomfortable.

"And?" Emmy asked, passing Jennifer a handful of tissues from the box on the nightstand. She didn't look particularly happy either, but she'd clearly been schooled in the art of sympathy by somebody who understood how to express it.

"And my grandpop's the church pastor. His faith means everything to him."

"I'm sure you mean more."

Jennifer shook her head, and there was no mistaking the sadness in her eyes. "After my mom died, Grandpop and I had an argument. I told him I'd lost my faith in God, and he said his was the only thing he had left."

"Sometimes, people say things they don't mean in the heat of the moment."

"Not this time. He was furious when I left for New York. He said I'd handed my soul to the devil, and he'd never been so disappointed in me. But Mom always told me to follow my dreams, so I came anyway. Except

Grandpop was right. Now I'm stuck in a nightmare of my own making, and he hasn't called once since I got here."

"Have you tried calling him? He might be more understanding than you think."

"I never knew what to say. And how can I speak to him now? I mean, he's a founding member of the Purity Coalition."

"The what?"

"The Purity Coalition. They preach total abstinence before marriage. Oh gosh, if his congregation see me in those pictures, he'll die from shame. And I'll never be able to show my face back home again."

Ana had come across a man like that once, a long time ago in Russia. A priest who'd demanded both abstinence and obedience from his flock. Not only had he objected when an acquaintance of Zacharov's wanted to build a factory near his church, but he'd done so quite vociferously, hence Ana's involvement. The photos she'd taken were buried deep in the *kompromat* file, and the pastor was buried in a shallow grave on the outskirts of Nazarovo. Back then, the general hadn't been quite such a monster, and a shred of decency had lurked within his soul. When he saw the pictures of Father Konstantin in bed with his underage mistress—underage by about a decade—Zacharov had taped the man's eyelids open and forced him to watch as he removed both balls and his dick, one slice at a time.

Men like Father Konstantin were yet another reason Ana hated to let Tabby out of her sight.

"Growing up, I was under so much pressure to stay pure, and I promised I would," Jennifer continued.

"*Promised*. Like, in church, on my knees. But then I moved to New York, and it's a whole other world." Jennifer sniffled a bit and wiped at her eyes. "If I could pay the money, I would, but my credit cards are already maxed out just from living here, and I can't get a loan. I already tried everything. This is God's punishment, isn't it?"

"I can't speak on His behalf, honey, but you shouldn't pay," Emmy told her. "If you do, there's nothing to stop this asshole from coming back for more."

"Oh my gosh." Jennifer's mouth formed a perfect O. "I didn't even think of that. Why did I ever leave Red Oak Ridge? Honestly..." She gave a tiny hiccup, and her eyes filled with tears. "Honestly, I wish you'd never found me."

"I'm not sure dying would help. He could still send the pictures."

"I know that! Do you think I don't know that? I wrote him an email. It was my last hope. It's timed to send on Sunday evening, and I said I was gone and begged him to delete everything. I thought that if he realised what he'd done, he might show some compassion."

"I doubt it." Emmy shrugged. "People like that are selfish fuckers. Compassion's just a word in the dictionary to them."

"See?" The tears spilled over and cascaded down Jennifer's cheeks. "It's useless. There's nothing I can do."

"No, but there's plenty *I* can do. What's this prick's name? Do you have his number? Any idea where he lives?"

"He said he was called Trey, but I don't think that's his real name. In his first message, he introduced himself as 'the man you know as Trey.' But what can *you* do? He said if he got even a hint of the police sniffing around, he'd send the pictures right away."

"How do you contact him?"

"Always by email. Just an anonymous webmail address."

"We'll need copies of those messages. Where's your phone?"

"You're not really going to look for him, are you? You can't! What if he's dangerous?"

"We promise we'll be careful. Right, Ana?"

"We're always careful. Tell us everything you know about him."

"I..."

"Look, we can do this the hard way or the easy way," Emmy said. "Fuckers like that shouldn't get away with blackmail, so letting this go isn't an option." She flashed a sudden grin. "If you help us, we might even catch him by Sunday night."

Jennifer twisted the sheet in her hands. This wasn't the kind of decision she was used to making, Ana could tell. Over the years, coached by Zacharov and an army of psychologists, she'd become adept at reading people, at joining the dots of their personalities from a few minutes of observation and snippets of information. The only person she'd failed spectacularly with was Sam, but in a strange and sometimes awful way, that had turned out to be for the best.

An educated guess said Jennifer had grown up sheltered but felt stifled by life in a small town in general and by her family in particular. The move to

New York had been an opportunity to experiment, but she was naïve, too trusting, and she'd been stung in the worst possible way for a girl with her background.

The question was, would she trust Emmy?

Finally, Jennifer came to a decision. "I'd tell you about Trey, but I hardly remember anything." Her voice dropped again, an indicator of an admission she didn't want to make. This girl was an open book. An easy mark. "I was drinking that Friday night. One of the girls from the theatre said the bar was a great place to meet guys, nice guys, smart, not the kind of men my mom warned me about. And she hooked up with an accountant. His pickup lines were real cheesy, but he seemed nice."

"Was she there when you met Trey?" Emmy asked.

Jennifer shook her head. "She'd just left when he came in. I was about to leave too, but then he told me I looked like the girl he'd been waiting for all his life. I can't believe I fell for that."

Ana couldn't either.

"He kept buying me cocktails," Jennifer continued. "And I thought he was so kind. When he laughed, his eyes crinkled at the corners, and I kidded him he'd have wrinkles before he was thirty."

"See? You *can* remember. We know he's under thirty with laughter lines. That's more than we had two minutes ago. Can you recall what colour hair he had?"

"Brown. Quite dark, I think, although that might've been the lighting."

"If we brought in a sketch artist, could you describe his face?"

"I don't think so. Everything else is kind of fuzzy."

"Okay. Any tattoos? Piercings? Birthmarks?"

"I don't think so. He was sort of...plain. Unmemorable, I think, even without the alcohol."

"What was he wearing?"

"Beige pants and a button-down shirt. A pink one. I kidded he was in touch with his feminine side, and he said that all good men should be." Asshole. "Wait! He had a mark on his neck. Some sort of blue paint. I asked him about it, and he said he was an artist, and I said so was I, but then he started quizzing me about my job before I could ask anything more."

"That's okay—it's a start. Which bar did you meet him in?"

"The Clockwork Apple. It's near Penn Station."

"With a name like that, I'm sure we can find it."

There was a rush of air as the door to Jennifer's room got pulled open, and Emmy and Ana both whirled around. A nurse stood in the doorway, and she didn't look happy.

"Ms. Fleming's awake? You were supposed to call us if you noticed any changes."

"Ohmigosh!" Emmy's hands flew to her cheeks. "I'm so, so sorry. She just opened her eyes and started talking, and I clean forgot."

"Well, it's a good thing I'm here now, isn't it?" She elbowed Emmy out of the way and leaned over the bed. "How do you feel, hon?"

"Uh, tired?"

"There's somebody waiting to speak with you, okay? Dr. Felton is a wonderful listener."

"I'm not sure—"

"And I'm afraid your sister and cousin will need to leave until you've been checked over. They can come back later."

"My...sister? Oh, right...my sister. Yes."

Emmy looped her arm through Ana's and backed towards the door. "Just rest, honey. We'll see you in a bit. Want me to bring takeout? Hospital food's never up to much."

"I don't think I could eat anything."

Emmy's smile grew wider. "Shame. Guess there'll be more left for me."

CHAPTER 7

OUT IN THE parking lot, Emmy stuffed her phone into her pocket. The rain had stopped, but puddles dotted the asphalt and the place smelled of bad drains.

"We're going to the bar now?" Ana asked. "It's open till four a.m."

She'd checked out The Clockwork Apple's website while Emmy spoke to Bradley. The place was painfully modern, filled with hipsters and dry ice and neon lights powered by a rooftop wind turbine. The cocktails came in recycled jam jars, and the bar snacks were both vegan and organic. On Monday nights, they hosted New York's first "Silent Shindig," where revellers listened to music through headphones and anything above a whisper was banned.

Thankfully, talking was allowed on Fridays.

"Might as well."

"And Tabby's definitely asleep?"

"Apparently she passed out right after they got back. Bradley's promised to fix her hair as soon as she wakes up tomorrow."

Of course he had. Emmy had promised to confiscate his Platinum Amex if he didn't.

"Is Cade staying the night?"

"Yup. And Bradley's roped Ishmael into fetching Jennifer's phone. One of the other make-up girls took it home for safekeeping. Where are all the cabs? You'd think there'd be a bunch outside the hospital."

"Maybe we should stop at home first? We're not exactly dressed for a nightclub."

"Tabby's fine."

Busted. "*Da*, I know, but—"

"Here, I'll sort your outfit."

Before Ana could blink, Emmy had a knife in her hand, half-hidden, a black-bladed Emerson CQC-6B. Her favourite. When she lunged forward, Ana went for an armlock, but Emmy sidestepped, laughing.

"Stop being so touchy."

"What the fuck are you doing?"

"Bradley assures me ripped jeans and torn shirts are all the rage right now."

"I don't like holes in my clothes."

"If we're being picky, that sweater's mine. And don't worry—for every item of clothing I wreck, two more magically appear in its place."

Ana blocked another attempt on Emmy's part. "Fine, but I want to get back to the apartment quickly."

"Don't we all? I've still got a bloody headache."

A man's voice came out of the darkness. "Is everything okay?"

Ah, *gavno*. A knife fight in the hospital parking lot probably wasn't the best idea, no matter how innocent it might be, and they didn't need a Good Samaritan stepping in. Ana plastered on a smile. Would she ever master that expression?

"Very good, thank you. My sister's just slightly drunk."

"You're sure you don't need help?"

"I'm sure. Do you know where we can find a cab?"

"There's a taxi stand out on the street."

Half an hour later, they stood outside The Clockwork Apple. Emmy's knees were pale through the holes in her jeans, and Ana had cut a deep V in her sweater, exposing the edges of the silk bra Sam had bought her two weeks ago. He often came home with little gifts— underwear, knives, books and the like—although her favourite days were the ones when he arrived with takeout.

The place was strangely quiet for a city bar. Patrons sat around on mismatched stools, many of them drinking from hollowed-out apples and the aforementioned jam jars or eating presumably organic snacks from tiny silver bowls while soft music played in the background. So...civilised. Ana eavesdropped on the nearest conversation and found the group having a debate about philosophy. In New York. On a Friday night. Wow. These people really knew how to live. Perhaps the previous incarnation of her sweater would've been appropriate after all? Or maybe something with tweed or corduroy.

Sure, Ana had spent plenty of time debating philosophy back in Russia, but never in bars. Bars were for dancing or drowning your sorrows, depending on the circumstances. And most of her debates had been with General Zacharov, which meant they'd been somewhat combative since they'd both hated to lose. One time, they'd stayed up till five a.m. "discussing" which US city presented the most strategically important target for terrorists. Ana argued for

Washington, DC, because who wouldn't want to take out the White House, but the general insisted on New York because politicians did so little work, nobody would miss them if they all disappeared. Hit Wall Street, he said, and that would have a far bigger impact worldwide. Perhaps that was another reason Ana was twitchy this weekend.

In some ways, she missed the murderous old bastard's company, although she'd never admit that to anyone. She hated even admitting it to herself.

Ana took a better look around, this time assessing the bar itself. One double door at the front, an emergency exit to the left, and a single door at the rear on the right-hand side next to the bar. No sprinkler system. Was that a fire-code violation? Probably. Should there be a gunfight, there was cover behind the bar and several sturdy wooden tables that looked as if they came from reclamation yards. And security cameras lurked in each corner. Their field of view would give blind spots near the restrooms at the back and also to the side of a particularly ugly potted palm, but most of the interior was covered.

"Hmm..." Emmy said. "Normally, I'd offer the bartender a few quid to leave us alone with the CCTV footage for an hour, but he seems like the kind of guy who'd insist on a warrant first."

"Law student?"

"Worse. Sanctimonious prick."

Just what Ana needed in the early hours of the morning, but she had to agree with Emmy's assessment. Ana had met that type of guy a hundred times the world over. Been bored to tears by him on more than one occasion. But since giving up wasn't an option, that left them with one decision to make.

"Which of us gets the short straw?"

"Finding the tapes?"

"No, staying here in the bar to play lookout."

A guy sidled up to Emmy and interrupted the conversation. "I was wondering if you had an extra heart? 'Cause mine just got stolen."

"Has that line ever actually worked on anyone?" she asked.

The guy got all pouty, kind of like Bradley did when he didn't get his own way.

"Who gave you a sense-of-humour bypass?"

"Oh, I'm sorry. Should I be laughing at you?"

"Bitch."

If they hadn't needed to keep a low profile, Ana would've shown him just what a bitch *she* could be, but she bit her tongue instead. Emmy gave her head a little shake.

"Okay, I see your point about the short straw. Do you want to get the tapes? I saw the way you looked at that asshole, and we don't want any accidents."

"How did I look at him?"

"Like you wanted to spike his testicles on an ice pick."

Ana had been thinking of a bamboo skewer, but an ice pick would do. "Fine. I'll get the tapes."

Always the good little Girl Scout, Emmy carried a miniaturised comms system in her purse for emergencies, and now she slipped Ana an earpiece. Ana stuck it in her ear then fluffed her hair to hide the evidence.

Stolen-Heart Guy had moved to the other end of the bar to try his luck on a blonde who'd just walked in.

The men in The Clockwork Apple outnumbered the women, although there was what appeared to be a bachelorette party drinking cocktails in the corner nearest the door. It was easy to tell who was single. They hovered around each other, waiting for the right moment to go in for the kill like some primitive mating dance. Why had Jennifer come to a place like this? Did girls really find this fun?

Ana waited until Emmy waved the barman over, then slipped through the door at the back. Paused. Listened. At that stage, it would be easy enough to claim she'd gotten lost on the way to the bathroom. There wasn't much out the back—just a storeroom plus a tiny break area with an office attached. Another door led off the break room, that one marked with an exit sign—presumably it led to the service alley. The Clockwork Apple kept it simple with drinks and bar snacks—no hot food, and there was no kitchen. No cameras in the staff areas either, and the place was deserted.

So far, so good. Now, where was the computer that ran the cameras in the public section? The office looked like the best bet. The place had an old-style wired system, not a hi-tech wireless setup that transmitted remotely.

There was only one computer in the room, an ancient desktop hooked up to a dusty flat-screen. Huh. From the hipster scene out front, Ana had expected a MacBook at the very least. Still, someone had helpfully jotted the password on a Post-it note stuck to the front of the monitor, so that was something to be thankful for.

The software wasn't hard to find her way around.

Back in Russia, Ana had spent time with the GRU's cyber warfare unit, a building full of military geeks located a stone's throw from the Kremlin, and they'd taught her the basics she needed to know to extract information in the field. Of course, technology was always evolving, but perhaps Blackwood's tech team could keep Ana up to date?

Wait. She didn't *need* to keep up to date on hacking. New Ana should be using the internet to fill out preschool applications and order groceries. But old Ana... Much as she tried to deny it, old Ana still lurked inside.

Out in the bar, Emmy had ordered a Cosmopolitan. She might have been drinking earlier, but Ana knew that this cocktail was just for show. She'd nurse it at the bar while she kept an eye on the comings and goings and tried not to get distracted by men who couldn't read her "leave me alone" body language.

"Are you religious?" Ana heard one guy ask. "Because you're the answer to my prayers."

"Oh my gosh, yes!" Emmy said. "Take a seat. I'll buy you a non-alcoholic beer and we can talk about the Lord our Saviour. I think I actually have some pamphlets in my purse."

"Uh, sorry. I must have the wrong person."

"Hey! Where are you going? Haven't you found Jesus yet?" The guy must have gone out of earshot because she muttered, "Prick," under her breath.

"Hang in there," Ana told her. "I'm just finding the right files."

Friday night, two weeks ago... There they were. Ana still carried a thumb drive on her key ring out of habit, plus a high-capacity memory card in her wallet for those little emergencies. She jammed the drive into the USB slot, then sat back as the files began to copy. Why did this part have to be so fucking slow?

"Trouble coming in your direction," Emmy said softly. "A waitress."

Thirty percent done.

Ana slipped off the chair and crouched behind the desk. She wasn't worried about getting out of there, but she needed the damn files first. The door to the break room opened, and footsteps walked in Ana's direction. Stopped. Would a waitress need the computer? Probably not unless she needed to order stock or something.

Ana heard the sucking sound of a fridge door opening, the gurgle of a coffee machine as it dispensed a drink. Then a female voice, high-pitched, kind of whiny.

"I don't know what to do about Tyler. He keeps calling me, like, every hour, but Monica said I should leave him hanging for a while."

She was on the phone. Fantastic.

"No, he says it's totally over with her... I mean, I thought I loved him, but Instagram doesn't lie."

Yes, it did. All the damn time, in fact. But the girl kept twittering on, and Ana gathered her ex-boyfriend had cheated with a lifestyle blogger who'd posted pictures of the pair of them at a boutique hotel in Maine. First, he claimed they were just friends, then he said he made a mistake. A mistake was a drunken kiss in a bar, not a dirty weekend in Lewiston, yet the waitress was seriously considering getting back together with him?

Worse, whoever was on the other end of the line

seemed to be encouraging her. Some friend.

Since the vapid idiot appeared to be paying attention to nothing but her failed love life, Ana risked getting to her knees. Ninety percent done.

"OMG! Tyler's calling right now. What should I do? Should I answer? I don't know... I don't know... Oh, he hung up."

One hundred percent. Finished. Thank goodness. Ana quickly erased tonight's footage then deactivated the camera system. No one was gonna start a manhunt over someone accessing a computer, but there was no point in leaving evidence of her and Emmy's presence if they didn't need to. Second nature meant Ana had pulled on a pair of gloves as soon as she entered the break area, so there were no fingerprints.

The waitress's jaw dropped as Ana walked out of the office.

"Who are you? You're not supposed to be in there."

"Don't worry; I'm leaving. And take my advice— show some self-respect and kick Tyler's cheating ass to the kerb."

If it had been Ana he'd cheated on, she'd have kicked his ass off a mountain, but she didn't recommend that solution to everyone. Getting a slimeball up a mountain wasn't easy, for one thing, especially if he was unconscious.

By the bar, Emmy had been cornered by a guy with a bushy beard and a waxed moustache. If he stood any closer, he'd be in her lap.

"Was your dad a boxer?" he asked her. "Because damn, you're a knockout."

She glanced across and saw Ana coming. "Yeah, actually he was. I'm not even kidding. And if you don't get out of my way, I'll show you what an excellent right hook I have."

"Hey, I was just being friendly."

"No, you weren't. Cheesy, yes. Sleazy? Definitely. Next time you try that line on a girl, don't stand so close that she can smell the onions you had for dinner."

Emmy didn't bother waiting for him to move. She shoulder-checked him as she pushed past, just in time because the waitress had finally come to her senses and hung up the phone.

"Stop her!" She pointed at Ana. "She was in the office."

Everybody stared, but nobody moved as they strolled out onto the street. Emmy stuck her arm out and waved down a passing cab.

"Aren't you going to ask if I got the footage?" Ana said.

"No need. You're the legend that is Lilith. Of course you got the footage."

CHAPTER 8

"THERE'S OUR GUY."

Emmy was right. Trey or whatever his name was stood at the bar with Jennifer, both of them drinking from hollowed-out apples. Same bartender, same preppy crowd, same stilted atmosphere. Trey fit right in, dressed in a pair of chinos and a button-down shirt just as Jennifer had said, complete with a blue splodge peeking out from under the collar.

The question was, how did they find him?

Ana picked up another slice of pizza and bit into the thick, gooey mozzarella. Emmy had a sweet tooth, but if Ana had the choice of giving up chocolate or cheese, the chocolate would have to go.

They'd picked up the pizzas on the way back to Emmy's apartment on the Upper East Side because neither of them wanted to attempt cooking and the fridge was empty. Before they left Virginia, Bradley had offered to stock the kitchen with groceries, but since they were only meant to be in New York for four days, Emmy had told him not to bother.

But now, it seemed as if one of them might need to stay longer to sort out the Jennifer mess, and with Emmy booked on jobs next week, Ana realised it would have to be her. Weirdly, she looked forward to it. The prospect of using the skills she'd spent a lifetime learning for good rather than to do the bidding of a power-hungry general... Yes, she liked that idea.

As long as she could get help with Tabby, of course, and she'd need to borrow resources from Blackwood's New York office to assist with tracking down Trey. Cade, perhaps? Emmy seemed to think he was competent, and he'd got Tabby safely back home earlier. Ana had checked on her when they arrived, and she was sleeping peacefully in a king-sized bed in one of the guest rooms.

Now Cade picked up his own slice of pizza and gave a quiet snort.

"The Clockwork Apple, huh? That place is a stalking ground for intellectuals who can't get girlfriends."

"You've been there?" Emmy asked him.

"Made the mistake of going with a group from the office a few months back. Someone had coupons. Nerds kept hitting on Cassidy with bad pickup lines until Danny sat her on his lap, then Jackson got in a fight with some dweeb who accused him of being a misogynist because he called the waitress 'darlin'.'"

"An actual fight?"

"Yup. Jackson said, 'It was nothing personal, snookums,' and the asshole took a swing at him."

"How badly did the guy get hurt?"

"Knocked himself out when he tripped over a chair."

It was Emmy's turn to snort. "So, judging by his choice of hangout, Trey was a dick even before he started blackmailing Jennifer."

"Blackmail? Is that what this is about? I figured it was a bad breakup or something."

"I guess we should start this story from the

beginning."

"Wait for me!" Bradley squealed from behind them, rushing into the living room in a silk dressing gown. Judging by the wet hair and floral smell, he'd just got out of the tub. And he had what looked like mud plastered all over his face. "What happened?"

"Well, Jennifer—"

"Don't leave anything out."

"Jennifer—"

"I want every detail. I mean, this trip was my idea, and I deserve some credit for that."

"If I could get a word in edgeways..."

"Quit stalling."

When Bradley shut up for longer than a second, Emmy recounted the story, from finding Jennifer in the bathroom to her confession at the hospital to getting the video of Trey from the bar. Bradley's disgusted face said he shared Cade's view of The Clockwork Apple.

"Why would someone take her to that place? I'll get Ishmael to have a word with the cast. There're hundreds of better places to go in New York." He leaned closer to peer at Emmy's laptop screen. "Is that the guy? He doesn't look like a criminal."

"He's hardly gonna have 'blackmailer' tattooed across his forehead, is he? Although that's not a bad idea for when we catch up with him..."

"Should we get the forensics team to go to Jennifer's apartment?" Cade asked. "There might be fingerprints left. Or DNA."

"That seems like a sensible place to start. Me and Ana have two days left in New York, so we can head back to the area near Penn Station and ask around at more bars. The way the guy did this—it was smooth.

Practised. I'd put money on him having done it before."

And Ana had no doubt he'd keep doing it unless they caught him.

"I'll stay longer," she said quietly.

Emmy raised an eyebrow. "You will?"

"*Da*. We'll work something out. Sam will understand. I can't make cakes for shit, anyway."

A small smile played at the corners of Emmy's lips as she nodded once.

"Good, so we have a plan. Tomorrow..." She glanced up at the ornate clock on the wall. It was well past midnight. "Today, we'll look for evidence at Jennifer's place in the morning, then hit the bars in the evening. Which leaves the afternoon free. Trey told Jennifer he was an artist, so perhaps we could try visiting galleries or something? Bradley, you know the New York art scene better than any of us—where would painters hang out?"

"I don't know any painters who are assholes. Did he say what style he works in?"

"Nope. But I'm guessing it must be something modern if he's working in neon blue." Emmy pointed at Trey's neck in the still on the screen. "That apparently came from an art accident."

"Really? Hmm... Are you sure?"

"Right now, we're not sure of anything, but we have to start somewhere."

"Because I've only seen that particular shade of blue in one place recently, and it wasn't a gallery."

"Where?"

"Nigel went paintballing last month, and he got shot, like, ten times. Pink, green, orange, and blue, and the blue was that exact shade."

"Are *you* sure?"

"Oh, please. I know colour."

That much was true. Half of the times Ana had seen Bradley, he had some sort of swatches in his hand as he planned what to do to Emmy's home next. But who the hell got shot ten times at paintballing? Nobody from Blackwood, that was for sure.

"Who's Nigel?" Ana asked.

"Emmy's life coach."

Ana turned to her sister. "You have a life coach?"

"Not voluntarily. We rescued him from a kidnapper a while back, and now he just keeps showing up. He's dating Jed's wife's sister, so I can't get rid of him."

Jed was one of Emmy's ex-boyfriends, who she weirdly still got on with despite having split from him twice. He'd gotten married and fallen in love not so long ago. Yes, in that order.

Bradley put his hands on his hips. "Of course you can't get rid of Nigel. He's excellent at what he does. And you..." He poked Ana in the chest, then took a hurried step back when she glared at him. "You should speak to him too since your life's such a mess at the moment."

"My life is *not* a mess."

"You're a square peg trying to hammer yourself into a round hole. Your light doesn't shine anymore, and you should never let anyone dull your sparkle. I'll book you a session."

"No, I—"

The *beep beep beep* of Bradley's watch interrupted.

"Ooh, time to wash my face mask off. I'll call Nigel first thing in the morning."

He swished out of the living room, and Cade looked

as though he was trying to keep a straight face.

"What?" Ana asked.

"Uh, nothing." He quickly turned serious. "Sorry."

"So, paintball," Emmy said. Unlike Cade, she was still grinning. "Sounds more fun than visiting galleries, huh?"

Ana had to admit that it did. With paintball, they could become the Jackson Pollocks of the assassin world.

"*Da*."

"I'll get the research team to look into paintball centres. Surely there can't be that many in New York?"

"A few indoor ones," Cade offered. "Otherwise you have to go farther out."

"Have helicopter, will travel. Come on, let's get some rest."

CHAPTER 9

"WELL, THAT WAS easier than I thought," Emmy said, finishing her cup of coffee.

The forensics team hadn't even finished in Jennifer's apartment when Blackwood's research team emailed with a link to a Facebook page. And there was Trey, front and centre in the second post from the top, grinning with a bunch of his buddies. Except his name wasn't Trey. It was Chad.

Looking for five people to play paintball this Sunday. Private sessions only at this time of year, minimum of ten people. Got five already—anyone want to take us on?

Ana smiled a rare natural smile. "I've never had a criminal issue an actual invitation to shoot at him before."

"Me neither. But how can we possibly pass this up? All we need is three more people and some guns."

"Have you been paintballing before?"

"Like to an actual paintball facility? No, but I've shot plenty of people with Simunition in training. Did you use that stuff in Russia?"

Ana shook her head. "No, always real bullets. General Zacharov said that if we died, we clearly weren't good enough."

And Ana *had* been good enough. Time after time, she'd come through training with little more than bruises, and secretly, she missed the adrenaline rush. The feeling of being pushed to the edge and surviving. A paintball game wasn't exactly on the same level, but it was better than going on a shopping trip with Bradley, or worse, having to sit through another fucking musical.

"Black used to take the same attitude with me, except he didn't genuinely want me to die. He broke my arm once, though."

"What? How?"

"Close-quarters combat accident. Hmm, he's going to be disappointed when he hears about our excursion. He'd love to shoot Chad, but he had to go to Canada this weekend."

"Can you get three other people?"

"Honey, once I explain the situation, people'll be lining up to help out. Hold on, I'd better message this dick before anyone else gets in ahead of us."

Emmy logged onto Facebook as Tiffany Brent, a twenty-nine-year-old PR assistant from Atlanta who loved dogs and yoga. The profile picture was a picture of her from the neck down in sportswear. Not a bad choice of bait for a slug like Chad.

"Who does your social media profiles?" Ana asked.

"Mack, mostly, but she wants to recruit someone to help."

"I do the photos," Bradley said, bustling in with Tabby on his hip. "I'm excellent at photos."

Ana checked her daughter over carefully. Yes, her hair was back to its normal mahogany, and all traces of glitter had disappeared. Ana had offered to bathe her, but Tabby had clung to Bradley's leg and said she wanted him to do it instead. The request would have been unthinkable three months ago, and logically, Ana should have felt devastated at the rejection, but weirdly, she felt kind of...comforted. How life had changed. For years, it had just been her and Tabitha, and while she loved her daughter more than anything, the relief at finally having help, first from Sam and then from her new circle of friends, let her breathe a little easier. She had a safety net now. They both did.

"Although that picture isn't even Emmy," Bradley continued. "It's Sofia."

Really? "Who's Sofia?"

"Emmy's ex-girlfriend."

What? "Girlfriend? As in *girlfriend*?"

Emmy shrugged. "Yeah. So?"

Vau. Okay. "I just didn't realise."

"Don't knock it till you've tried it. At least she didn't leave dirty laundry all over the floor."

Ana blew out a breath, remembering the state of the bedroom earlier in the week. She'd tried reminding Sam to put his clothes in the laundry hamper, but she might as well have been speaking Punjabi. He'd been messy back in Russia too. It was a good thing he made up for his untidiness in other ways.

And Emmy... It was hard having to learn about her so late in life. They should have been together as kids, should have grown up together. Damn their father for keeping them apart.

"I'm not sure I'll try it, but... What was she like?"

"As a person? Or...you know?"

Blyat', there was such a thing as too much

information. "As a person. Jeez."

"Uh...quirky?"

"Bipolar," Bradley muttered.

"She mostly keeps that under control."

"And she kills people."

"Only bad people."

"She's an assassin too?" Ana asked.

Emmy nodded. "Yup. You'll probably meet her someday."

"You still see her?"

"She's just finished doing some work for us, and now she's on vacation in the Cayman Islands. A shame she's not around really, because if she was, I'd invite her to join our paintball team. And speaking of paintball..."

Emmy turned back to her laptop and began to type.

Hey, are you still looking for people to play paintball? Me and some friends are in New York for my birthday this weekend, and it sounds like so much fun!

Tiffany x

While they waited for a reply, Emmy clicked through to Chad's profile. He wasn't an artist, he was a marketing assistant from Queens. Most of his posts were him drinking with his frat-boy buddies, flexing his mediocre muscles in the gym, or playing wannabe commando at the Mayhem Paintball Centre on Staten Island. He appeared to go there every other weekend, when he wasn't busy extorting women, that was.

"You found him, then?" Bradley said. "I knew you would. Are you gonna put real bullets in the paintball gun?"

"They're air guns. They can't fire real bullets. Besides, I think we want to have a bit more fun with him than that."

The laptop pinged. It seemed Chad kept a close eye on his phone.

Chad: How many of you are there?

Tiffany: Six. But Cindi's not feeling so good after last night, so she might stay at the hotel.

Chad: Ever played paintball before?

Tiffany: No, but we're fast learners.

Chad: Can you get to Staten Island by 10 o'clock?

Tiffany: Tomorrow?

Chad: Yeah, tomorrow.

Tiffany: We can totally get there tomorrow. I swear we won't even be hungover. Do we need to bring anything?

Chad: All the equipment's provided. Just wear clothes you can run in.

Tiffany: Like joggers?

Chad: Something tighter works better. Look forward to meeting you, Tiffany.

Something tighter? Sleazeballs were so predictable. Ana had always preferred looser-fitting combat pants for jobs like this one, but she'd make a special effort to dress up for Chad. By lulling him into a false sense of security, victory would be so much sweeter.

But they still had one small part of the plan to finalise.

"We need three more people. Who should we ask?"

"Easy," Emmy said. "Carmen, Dan, and Mack."

"I thought Mack did computers?"

"She's actually pretty well trained in combat as well, and it's good for her to get away from her screens every so often. Eye strain and all that." Emmy was already tapping away at her phone, and soon ringing sounded through the speaker. "Carmen? Is it possible to fire a tranquilliser dart from a paintball gun?"

"I can't say I've ever tried it, but what are you planning? Sounds like fun."

Carmen was a sniper, formerly of Mexico's GAFE High Command. Her superiors hadn't been happy when she married Black's best friend on a whim and emigrated to America. To this day, Blackwood gave the Mexican special forces a discount on their services to make up for stealing her.

"We're teaching a blackmailer the error of his ways. What are you doing tomorrow?"

"Seems I'm shooting a blackmailer with a tranquilliser dart."

"Then you think it can be done?"

"They're both air guns. I'll get Luther onto it."

Luther was Blackwood's armourer. Ana had only met him once, at headquarters, where he hung out in the basement within spitting distance of the underground firing range. Said he liked the peace and quiet. If Carmen was Blackwood's hotshot, Luther was the master at facilitating her deadly games.

"Lovely. And could you go into the vault at Riverley and get me a vial marked…uh…" Emmy consulted a note on her phone. "G207-b."

"What is it?"

"No idea, but Sofia assures me it'll bring down a horse."

"Tell me we're not shooting a horse as well."

"Nope, just people. I'll call her and find out the appropriate dose. And can you bring Dan and Mack with you? I'll send the helicopter."

There was a pause, and Ana pictured Carmen rolling her eyes. "Anything else?"

"Do you still have Josh's 'It's my birthday!' button? The one he wore at his last party?"

"Uh, probably?"

"Great, can you bring it?"

"Is that all?"

"Yeah, I'm pretty sure that's everything."

CHAPTER 10

"HOW ARE YOU feeling?" Emmy asked Jennifer.

Since they didn't have to spend Saturday afternoon hunting for Chad, Ana and Emmy went to the hospital to check on Jennifer instead. It was either that or go to an art gallery with Bradley.

Not that Ana had anything against art, but this was the modern stuff, and when Emmy had looked up the details of the show over breakfast, the main installation consisted of a woman wearing her clothes inside out while she stared at seventeen TVs. According to the blurb, *Seeing Blind* demonstrated the dysfunctionality of modern society, and just looking at a snapshot of it reinforced Ana's decision to leave the television switched off whenever Sam was out. She wanted Tabby to experience life for herself, not watch it through somebody else's eyes.

Jennifer held up her bandaged wrists. "The doctor says it could've been worse. Apparently, I cut in the wrong direction. Couldn't even get that right."

"And up here?" Emmy tapped her head.

There was a long pause, the silence filled by groaning from a man on a gurney in the hallway.

Finally, Jennifer admitted, "I'm scared."

"Did you speak to the psychologist?"

"She suggested calling the police, but there's only a

day left until Trey's deadline. The doctors can't tell my grandpop, can they?"

"Not if you don't want them to."

"How can I get out of here? I want to leave, but they say I can't go home without a safety plan. But I don't need a freaking safety plan—I need Trey's testicles in a damn vice!"

A vice? How heavy were those? Perhaps a small portable version... Ana flexed her fingers. No, on second thought, she'd manage just fine. And Jennifer appeared better too—anger was an improvement on tears any day.

"Don't worry about Trey," Emmy said, smirking. "Everything's in hand." In hand? Seemed she'd had the same thought. "Although perhaps the safety plan isn't a bad idea. What's it all about?"

"Like, a set of steps I can follow if I feel suicidal again. I need activities to distract myself and people I can talk to. But I hardly know anybody in New York, so they want to keep me here running up medical bills I can't afford."

"Don't worry about the medical bills. And I'm your sister, remember? Let's have a talk with your doctors and see if we can get you released."

Four hours later, the three of them walked into the chilly winter air. As part of the bargain Jennifer had struck with Emmy over the safety plan, she'd agreed to keep seeing a therapist. Her cracks ran deeper than the suicide attempt—she still hadn't processed her mom's death properly, and she seemed to have self-esteem issues too. Was that why she hid behind make-up? Masks came in many different forms.

But for now, Jennifer was free. Emmy's apartment

was going to be full to bursting tonight. It had four bedrooms, but with Emmy having to sleep alone for safety reasons when she wasn't on a challenging job, someone would be taking the sofa.

"Wow," Jennifer breathed when they walked through the front door. "You live here? I thought you were kidding about having a place on the Upper East Side."

"Live here? Not really. But I stay here occasionally." Laughter and the *clink* of glasses sounded from the living room. "Sounds like the girls have arrived."

Jennifer's head swivelled right and left as they walked through the apartment, taking in all the details, which was kind of the same reaction Ana had had when she first arrived, except she liked to think she'd been slightly more subtle about it. She did have a reputation to protect, after all, and that reputation didn't involve going gaga over the marble-floored entrance hall, the fitness room with its views of Central Park, the roof terrace, or the living room bigger than the whole of the apartment she'd shared with Sam in Russia. According to Bradley, Black's grandfather had bought the post-war Manhattan building in the sixties, and now Emmy and Black rented out the other three apartments while keeping the top floor as a pied-à-terre.

A fourteen-million-dollar pied-à-fucking-terre.

The pair of them were generous with the keys— generous with everything they owned, in fact—but more than once, Ana had mused over their lifestyle. They didn't live in the real world. And right now neither did she, which was why she still pinched herself.

Rather than eating in the dining room, the girls had

spread the food out on the coffee table in the living room and part of the floor too. A picnic, Upper East Side-style. Dan leapt up to hug Emmy, then embraced Ana a little more gingerly. Ana wasn't sure she'd ever get used to the hugging thing.

"We ordered Chinese."

"And Italian, and Mexican," Mack added.

And ice cream, by the looks of it. Tabby was up to her elbows in the stuff, and she'd got rainbow sprinkles all over the carpet, but she was smiling so much Ana couldn't even be mad.

"*Kotyonak*, you're making a mess."

"Bradley bring ice cream."

"Don't worry," he said. "We need a new carpet."

Emmy closed her eyes and took a steadying breath. "Bradley, we don't need a new carpet. This *is* a new carpet. So far, every footstep on it's cost about fifty dollars."

"I guess maybe we could get it shampooed."

"Great idea. Guys, meet Jennifer. She's gonna be staying here with us tonight."

Dan squashed the breath out of her too. "Come and eat. Bradley ordered enough for the entire building plus everyone passing on the street too."

Shell-shocked. That was a good way to describe Jennifer as she tiptoed into the living room. Carmen patted the sofa next to herself.

"Plenty of room here. Do you like tacos?"

And the ice was broken. "Everybody likes tacos."

Helping people... It felt good.

CHAPTER 11

CHAD AND HIS buddies circled the Blackwood girls like sharks. Not great whites, more baby tiger sharks—they wanted to be tough, but they just didn't have the teeth for it. Ana might have felt sorry for them if Jennifer's blood-covered body weren't quite so fresh in her mind. And also if she hadn't been forced to give up part of her vacation to teach Chad that extorting innocent girls had consequences. Not that she minded playing paintball for a couple of hours—on the contrary, she was starting to miss her regular shooting practice—but it was more a matter of principle. Ana was used to going after lions. Chad was an insect, a pesky gnat who didn't deserve her time.

At least Tabby hadn't been bothered by Ana's departure at the crack of dawn. Bradley had mentioned something about baking, and she'd practically tripped over her feet running to the kitchen. Well, rather him than Ana—Bradley knew how to operate a stove, according to Emmy, so at least there wouldn't be a repeat of the fire extinguisher incident.

The pricks introduced themselves—Tad, Brad, whatever—but during last night's planning session in the master suite, Dan had christened Chad's sidekicks douchebros one through four, and the nicknames stuck.

"You ever shot a gun before?" Chad asked Emmy-slash-Tiffany. She'd dressed for the occasion in skintight leather pants and plenty of eyeliner. Ana had worn Lycra, but the movie-villain make-up was a step too far for her. Jennifer had given her a more natural look, including a few extra eyelashes and perfectly applied mauve lipstick. Whatever the girl's mental state, her cosmetic skills were on point.

Emmy giggled. "No, never. Is it hard?"

She glanced at his crotch as she asked the question. Giggled again. The girls were older than the douchebro collective, but the assholes seemed to be viewing that as a challenge rather than a drawback. So far, so good.

"It's easy, babe. Let me show you."

He demonstrated how to refill the air tank of the paintball gun, or marker, as they were called, and fumbled a bit as he loaded more paintballs into the hopper—pink for the girls, blue for the boys. Then the referee came out to give a briefing, his breath steaming cold as he stamped his feet to get some warmth into them.

"Today, you're gonna be playing 'capture the flag.' Each team has a flag to hide in their territory, and the goal of the opposing team is to find that flag and bring it back to their base. Since there are only five of you on each side, we're gonna play a variant we like to call Zombie Paintball. Rather than a player being completely out of the game when she gets hit, she has to sit in timeout for sixty seconds instead. Then she gets to rejoin, like the undead. Get it?"

Oh, it was so cute the way he directed his comments at the girls' team.

"Where's timeout?" Dan asked.

"Right over here by my cabin. See that bench? A hit is a solid nickel-sized circle of paint on any part of your body or equipment. Spatter from a paintball hitting, say, a tree doesn't count. If you're not sure whether you've been properly hit, yell for a paint check, and we'll pause the game while I take a look."

"Surely we'll know if we've been hit?"

"Maybe not, if someone aims at your back. We've got good, solid body armour for you ladies to wear."

Except there would be no paint checks. The girls had their game plan, and the first thing Carmen would do was neutralise the ref. Nobody wanted to play by the pesky rules today.

"How long are we playing for?" Emmy asked.

"Forty minutes. But if you get tired, just say so, and we can take a break halfway."

A break? In warfare, there were no fucking breaks. And they'd need the full forty minutes to educate Chad in the ways of the world. This was so much more fun than shopping.

"Everybody ready to gear up?" the ref asked. "Or do you want me to go over anything again?"

"We're good," Emmy said, and the boys grinned and nodded too.

"How did you all meet?" Douchebro Number One asked Mack as they fastened themselves into body armour. It didn't fit very well, a far cry from the custom-made kit Ana had used on Blackwood's recent excursion to Russia. It was almost like being back with Zacharov. He'd thought sending her into battle in street clothes, armed with only a .22 and her fists, was character building.

"Oh, we were in the same sorority at college in

Atlanta," Mack answered. She was playing up her Texas accent today. Ana noticed she'd removed her wedding ring, as had Emmy and Carmen. Emmy had hers on a leather cord around her neck. Close to her heart, she said.

"Which sorority?"

"Beta Gamma Gamma," Ana told him. Bitches Got Guns. She'd been practising her American accent since she arrived in the US, and now it seemed the efforts were paying off. "How about you? Chad said you were frat brothers."

"Delta Alpha Mew."

Dumb-Ass Motherfuckers?

"What was your major?"

"I played football. Yours?"

"Poli-sci."

Ana might not have been to college, but thanks to Zacharov, she knew more about politics, about the distribution of power and resources than anyone could learn from books. As England's Lord Acton once said, *Power tends to corrupt, and absolute power corrupts absolutely. Great men are almost always bad men.* Ana had seen the darkness in wealthy men the world over, in Zacharov himself, and even in Emmy's own husband.

"What do you do now?" the douchebro asked.

"I'm a waste management consultant."

"That's...interesting." His tone suggested it was anything but, and he turned to Dan. "What do you do?"

"Research and analysis." She shrugged. "It pays the bills. But in my spare time, I like to go pole dancing."

"Really?" The asshole's eyes lit up.

"Yeah, Poles are the best dancers. My dance

partner's called Pawel. He comes from Kraków." Ana had to stifle a laugh at the guy's disappointed expression. "Such a shame he's gay, because girls have needs, you know?"

Douchebro bobbed his head. "I do know. Need a hand with your jacket?"

"I'd *love* a hand."

"How do I put these knee pads on?" Mack asked.

DB Number Three was only too happy to help. "You've got them upside down, babe."

"People, are we ready?" the ref called. "Does everyone have their goggles on?"

They did, and their markers were loaded and ready. The ref held up an air horn, and a second later, it blasted to signal the start of the game.

The boys had a slight advantage in that they knew the terrain better than Team Blackwood, but the girls had got up early and arrived at the paintball field while it was still dark. They'd spent three hours mapping out the lie of the land, dividing the area into zones and working out the best spots for attack and cover while Mack complained about the cold. Three hours might not seem like much to cover twenty-five acres, but it was enough time for them to come up with a strategy, warm up in the car with a flask of coffee afterwards, then drive back around through the front gates as if they'd just arrived.

With the game underway, they split as planned, with Emmy and Ana running north and Mack and Dan heading south. Carmen would be on her own, as was usual for her as team sniper. The boys bolted in the opposite direction, and Emmy stopped to strip the flag off its pole and stuff it into her pocket. Good luck to

Team Douchebro in trying to find that. Ana fitted her comms gear while Emmy did the same, then they moved off again, more slowly this time.

The ground was frozen, and they had to tread carefully to avoid leaves crunching underfoot, flitting from tree to skeletal tree to stay out of sight. Evergreens were scattered among the tangle of undergrowth, and the paintball operators had built artificial cover in the form of bunkers and screens. The whole place was covered in brightly coloured paint, and Ana wondered if they should've let Bradley organise their outfits for the day. With his assistance, they'd probably have blended in better with the neon landscape.

"The ref's taking a nap," Carmen said over the radio. "I've locked him inside the cabin with the heater on. Luther's darts worked perfectly. The guy never knew what hit him, but we should probably send him some candy or something as an apology later."

Ana and Emmy grinned at each other. Objective one: complete. Now they could move on to objective two. Chad.

The sound of shooting erupted from the far side of the field as they swapped out their regulation goggles for slimline headsets designed by Carmen's husband, Nate. Four blue dots and one red one pulsed on the heads-up display, a pair and a trio. What? You thought Team Blackwood would play fair? Of course not. The secret to successful warfare was tilting the playing field in your direction before the battle even started. They'd tagged the other team with trackers while they got dressed, and with a tap on her smartwatch, Ana overlaid the white dots of Team Blackwood as well.

"Got one," Dan said. "He's gone to sit down."

Carmen spoke up. "I'll get him again on his way back."

Emmy chuckled. "We'll have to carve Chad away from his two buddies. Heading in your direction."

It was almost too easy to fall into step behind their opponents as they walked past, hit them up with a little of Sofia's magic potion, and drag them into nearby bunkers. They'd wake up groggy in a few minutes, minus their esteemed leader and ready for another round of target practice with Dan, Mack, and Carmen.

Now for Chad... He squealed as Ana dropped out of a tree and landed on top of him, bringing him to the ground in one smooth move. Emmy bound his wrists with flex cuffs before he realised what was happening, then hauled him to his feet.

"Walk."

"What the hell...?"

"Walk." She jabbed him in the kidneys with the barrel of her marker. "Or we'll drag you, but that'll piss us off and trust me, you don't want that."

"You can't do this! It's against the rules." He opened his mouth to yell, but Ana clapped a hand over it.

"Nobody's left to hear you, *dorogoy*." Ana had switched to a Russian accent, and Chad's eyes widened. "Scream if you want, but like Tiffany said, you don't want to piss us off."

"Who are you people?"

"I'm the fucking devil," Emmy said. "I just style my hair so the horns don't show."

Chad tried to make a break for it, but she kicked his legs out from underneath him and he landed in the dirt.

"Oh, don't go. We've barely gotten to know each other."

Emmy shoved Chad's camouflage-print bandana into his mouth then caught his arms, cursing when he jabbed at her with his cuffed hands. *Nice try, mudak.* Ana took his feet as they half carried, half dragged him to the edge of the paintball field, shoved him under the wooden fence, and hauled him upright on the other side. When they lashed him to a sturdy old oak with paracord, the faint smell of urine drifted from his pants. Poor baby was scared? Good.

He turned whiter when Emmy tugged the gag out of his mouth and dropped it on the ground.

"Okay, so here's the deal. We've heard you've been supplementing your income with a touch of blackmail?"

"I haven't! I don't know what you're talking about."

Emmy didn't bother to argue, just fished around in his pockets, avoiding the damp patch spreading from his crotch. He had the latest iPhone, and she held it up, smiling as it unlocked with the facial recognition feature.

"Let's see, shall we?"

She scrolled through the photos first, and no wonder Jennifer didn't want those going to her grandfather. Chad had taken more than just a few candid boudoir shots—she was tied to the bed, legs spread, and there was a video too. Emmy pressed play, turned the sound up, and held it in front of Chad's face.

"Does this ring any bells?"

He looked at his feet.

Emmy went through his emails next, her mouth

flattening in a thin line.

"Ten thousand bucks in Bitcoin by Monday or the pictures go to everyone. No delays, no excuses," she read. "Fuck, how many girls have you done this to?" She kept scrolling. "Four...five...six. Did they all pay up?"

Chad wasn't so talkative anymore. He tried to turn his head away, but Ana grabbed his face, digging her nails into his cheeks as she forced him to face Emmy.

"What, you didn't make enough money from your marketing job, so you started a side hustle? You're a worm, dude. The lowest of the fucking low. Which leaves us with a conundrum. When we only knew about the one girl, we planned to have a word and then let you go, but six? We could bury you out here, and no one would ever find the body."

"Please, I... Rent's expensive, okay?"

"You live on your own in a two-bedroom apartment, asshole. If money's a problem, get a smaller place or a roommate. For fuck's sake, you're an economics major. It's not really that difficult, is it?"

"Look, I'm sorry, I—"

"Lucky for you, we didn't bring a spade, so here's what we're gonna do. You're gonna write a heartfelt apology to each of the girls you blackmailed, and then you're gonna pay all the money back."

"I don't have fifty thousand bucks!"

"Sixty thousand."

"Sixty? The last girl didn't even pay up."

"You owe her compensation for mental anguish. And if you don't have the cash, you'd better find a way to get it, hadn't you? A legal way. You could start by selling your fancy paintball gear because by the time you get a third job, you won't have spare time to play games anyway." Face ID worked its magic again, and Emmy paged through Chad's bank transactions. "You spend way too much time in bars, dude. Eighteen grand and change left... We'll split that six ways to start with."

"No way. I have to live off that."

"If you behave, we'll give you the address of a soup kitchen before we leave. What's the password for your Blockchain account?"

Silence.

Ana ran the edge of her boot along Chad's shin, playing bad cop to Emmy's not-quite-so-bad cop. When he howled, she backhanded him.

"Password. Now."

He gave Emmy the password, and she cut his hands free then held out a pad and pen. "While I deal with the finances, you can write a nice note to each of your victims. Make sure you grovel."

When he didn't move to take the stationery, Ana whipped out her backup gun, and that one didn't fire paintballs. Hiding it had been a challenge, but Bradley had found her a nice loose jacket.

"Write."

Chad wrote.

The handwriting was kind of shaky, but he managed to scrawl out six apologies in the time it took Emmy to empty his bank account. Not exactly gushing, but they'd do. Emmy snapped a picture of each note and emailed them to their respective recipients.

"You still owe each of the girls seven thousand dollars. You've got six months to pay it."

"Six months? Are you crazy?"

"So people say."

"How the hell am I supposed to do that?"

"Get creative. We'll be checking in with the girls to make sure you're meeting your obligations, and if you don't, we'll pay you another visit. We found you once, and you'd better believe we'll find you again."

"But—"

Ana picked up her marker and fired a paintball into his crotch. His eyes bulged, and he would've doubled over if he hadn't been tied to the tree.

"If any of those pictures see the light of day, next time it will be a real bullet."

There was nothing more to be said. With his hands untied, Chad would eventually pick himself free—either that or his friends would find him and he'd have fun explaining the situation. It was time to leave.

"All done," Emmy murmured over the radio.

"So are we," Carmen replied.

None of the paint-splattered men sitting in timeout said a word as the girls stripped off their body armour and dumped it in a heap along with their weapons. It had been a rout. The douchebros wouldn't have looked out of place in *Glitter*.

Mack gave them one last backwards glance. "You know, that was actually fun. Maybe I *should* step out from behind my desk more often."

CHAPTER 12

"ARE YOU STAYING for lunch?" Emmy asked Cade. He'd come to the apartment to keep watch over Tabby and Bradley while Ana went out to have fun, but judging by the mess in the kitchen and the three empty coffee cups on the side table in the hallway, Bradley had spent the time helping Tabby to ice cookies while Cade hid out on the couch in the foyer. At least he'd maintained line of sight to the front door.

"I can't. Tia wants to go to some art gallery."

Tia was Mack's husband's little sister, and she and Emmy had been close until tragedy struck on Ana's last trip to Russia. Ana didn't have to be a genius to understand the toll the fallout had taken on Emmy. Tia had moved out of Emmy's house, all the way to New York where she was working for Bradley's friend Ishmael. Ana had been surprised when Tia didn't come to see *Glitter* with them, but when she'd asked, Emmy had shaken her head and said it wasn't the right time.

Now Cade was with Tia?

"Then you'd better go. I'll give you a ride to Tribeca."

"The subway's quicker."

"Sure?"

"Yeah, I'm sure."

Emmy nodded, her earlier good mood evaporated.

"Cade? Look after her, okay?"

"That's my job, boss."

His job? So Cade's interest in Tia was on a professional level rather than personal? Ana wasn't sure how the teenager would like having a bodyguard.

Cade saluted and headed for the door, and a moment after it closed behind him, Bradley rushed out of the living room with Tabby clinging to his back like a monkey.

"Oh." His brows knitted. "I thought that was the delivery guy with brunch."

"How can you have brunch? It's gone noon."

"Because brunch comes with champagne, and we have to celebrate. Jennifer just got an email from Trey. Did you make him send it?"

"We might have encouraged him, yes."

"Do you think he'll keep his word and delete the photos?"

"I deleted them from his phone. He could have backups, but..." Emmy glanced at Ana. "No, I don't think he'll send them to anyone."

Jennifer appeared in the doorway. "Did Bradley tell you? About the note?"

"Yes."

"I can't believe it! Grandpop always told me God fixes everything, but I'd stopped believing it was true." A hesitant smile spread across her face. "He came through."

"That wasn't God," Bradley told her. "That was Emmy and the girls."

"Huh?"

"We might've found Trey and had a word," Emmy said.

"Really? You found him?"

"He's very sorry."

Jennifer chewed on her lip for a moment, thinking. "Well, I still think God helped, because otherwise how did you find me in the first place?"

Ana was about to say "olfactory receptors" but Emmy got in first.

"Maybe you're right. Who knows? We can't explain everything that happens in the world, but I'm glad things worked out. How are your wrists today?"

"Better. Much better. Everything's better. This...this crushing weight...it's gone."

Ana knew that feeling too. When she left Base 13 for the final time, when she said goodbye to Russia, it was as if she could breathe again. But over the last couple of months while she played housewife, the atmosphere had become cloying, so gradually she barely noticed. Today, the air had cleared.

Life smelled sweeter.

"I... I think I should call Grandpop," Jennifer said. "I miss him, and I said some horrible things... Yes, I should call him."

"That's an excellent decision," Bradley said, passing Tabby to Ana. "Come with me, and I'll find you a quiet spot. Would you like a cup of herbal tea?"

As Jennifer followed Bradley out of the room, Ana realised the newcomer wasn't the only one with a big decision to make. This weekend had shown her that sticking with the status quo wasn't an option. Dreams changed, ambitions evolved. Yes, Ana had to give some serious consideration to her future too.

Jennifer was full of smiles as they headed out for the last of Bradley's planned excursions. Mack and Dan had escaped back to Richmond, but Carmen couldn't think up a good enough excuse, so she'd been dragged along to the New York Public Library too.

"You're an honorary auntie," Bradley explained. "It's important for you to spend time with Tabby."

"What about my own son? Shouldn't I be spending time with him?"

"You know as well as I do that Nate's taken him camping this weekend."

Carmen and Emmy may have been at the library under duress, but Jennifer seemed to be enjoying herself as they headed for a craft session in the kids' section. Ana? Well, the visit to the Children's Museum in Manhattan had been less painful than she'd feared, and she may even have joined in with feeding the goats at the petting zoo in Central Park. The best part, though, was watching Tabby have fun with the other kids. The day had been a reminder to Ana that following her instincts to keep her daughter isolated would most likely backfire and lead not only to resentment, but also to Tabby growing up naïve like Jennifer. No, Tabby needed to get out and experience life, no matter how uncomfortable being in public made Ana feel.

"Here we are," Bradley announced. "The Kraft Korner. Isn't it fabulous?"

Tabby ran towards a table full of glue, pens, paper, and fuck knew what else. *Please, say there isn't any fucking glitter.*

"Your little girl's so cute," Jennifer said to Ana. "Does she have any brothers or sisters? I taught Sunday school back in Red Oak Ridge, and I just loved all the children."

"No, Tabby's enough." *She's everything.*

"I always wanted at least three, but after Trey, I think I've been put off men for life."

"Don't let one man shape your worldview."

Emmy slung an arm around her shoulders. "Ana's right. There are great men out there, but from what I've seen, they don't hang out at The Clockwork Apple."

"No kidding."

"Next time you get a man's number, call me and I'll get him background-checked before you go on a date."

"You can do that?"

"Yup. Put it in your safety plan, okay?"

"I will." She turned her head away and looked down at her feet. "I still can't believe I have one of those. Or... or what I did. Something in me just broke that day."

"Stress does nasty things to a person's mind. All those little problems, they pile up until one day the dam breaks."

"What do you think everyone will say when I go back to work? I don't want them to treat me funny." She tugged her sleeves down over the bandages, something she'd done every few minutes since they left the apartment.

"Be honest with them. Explain that it was a difficult time and let them support you. Better to have backup than to try and cope alone."

"I might go and visit my grandpop for a few days."

They'd cleared the air now. Jennifer had been in

tears again after she called him, but Bradley had explained that they were good tears rather than bad ones. He knew what to do with the tissues, anyway, and a hot drink appeared to be soothing too. Ana made a mental note of that for the future, just in case she ever had to deal with another sobbing and/or hysterical woman. Apparently, Grandfather Fleming had wanted to call Jennifer for months, but he didn't know what to say—a trait that ran in the family, it seemed.

Emmy nodded. "I think a visit home is a great idea."

Tabby waved a tube of something in the air. "Jennfer! Help me."

The top popped off the tube, and glitter flew over everything. The table, the carpet, the other kids, some of the parents. Fuck.

Emmy backed away. "I've never seen that child before in my life."

"It's okay, I can fix that," Jennifer said, smiling brightly. "We just need some sticky tape. Has anyone got sticky tape?"

This was much better. The new café on the mezzanine floor at the library overlooked the craft area, and Ana, Emmy, and Carmen could watch Tabby making a mess while Bradley and Jennifer cleared it up. The distance made Ana a bit twitchy, but she could jump over the balcony if necessary. The bookshelves below were practically ladders.

"What better way to relax after paintball than with chocolate cake?" Emmy asked. "We should do this more often."

Carmen had ordered a cup of green tea and nothing else. "I'm still full after brunch."

"So am I. But the cake's got fresh cream filling and strawberries on the top, so it's basically health food."

"I'm not sure your nutritionist would agree."

"What he doesn't know won't hurt him."

Ana picked at her own food as Tabby laughed with the girl beside her. Yes, she was definitely having fun in New York, far more fun than she'd had wrapped up in darkness and cotton wool in Sam's apartment. Ana had to make the change, didn't she?

"You okay?" Emmy asked. "You've hardly touched that cookie."

"We *should* do this more often."

"Go to the library? Or eat cake?"

"No, I mean the whole trip."

Ana felt as though she'd achieved something over the weekend. The way they'd been able to help Jennifer. The sense of justice from giving Chad his just deserts. The teamwork.

"Oh, fuck. Bradley's corrupted you."

"I'm not talking about the shopping parts." No way. And not the musical parts either. "But look at Tabby— she's having a ball down there. And I enjoyed this morning more than I should have."

"Oh, thank goodness." Emmy grinned. "At last, you're realising what everyone else has known for ages. You need action or you get bored out of your mind."

"I'm the same," Carmen said. "When I first had Josh, I thought I'd be able to switch off from my old life and be a mom, but it just didn't work out that way. Neither of us is cut out to be a housewife."

"Don't you worry about Josh when he's not with you?"

"All the time, but he needs to have a life too. Right now, he's probably fishing with Nate, and last time, he fell into the lake because he leaned over the side of the boat and tried to catch a fish with his damn hands. They both stank when they got home, and on a hot day, the car still smells funny."

"Going back to work scares me," Ana whispered.

"That just proves you're human, no matter what people might say."

"So, what's it to be?" Emmy asked. "Want me to keep that desk for you at Blackwood?"

Sam had already suggested Ana should get out more, said that he'd support her with whatever she wanted to do. Espionage and action flowed in his blood too. He'd understand.

"Yes, I do. On one condition."

"Name it."

"You stop Bradley from calling Nigel. I don't need a fucking life coach."

Emmy laughed. "Deal. I'll distract him with a decorating project or something. Even if my house ends up pink from top to bottom, it'll be worth it."

With the decision made, Ana was finally able to relax. The cookie tasted like chocolate rather than dirt, and she planned out the questions she'd ask the principal of any prospective preschool. Tabby could have the life Ana had never had as a child, one filled with friends and laughter. She certainly seemed to be getting on well with her new buddy.

And... Ana nudged Emmy. "Do you see the way that guy next to Bradley is looking at Jennifer?"

"Like he wants to put her on a white horse and ride off into the sunset? Yeah."

Carmen sighed. "That's so sweet."

"Looks as if that background check's gonna be happening sooner than I thought. I love a happy ending."

And secretly, so did Ana's cold, dead heart.

WHAT'S NEXT?

My next book will be *Demented*, the fourth book in the Electi series, releasing in 2020.

Demented

Iris McGivern never envisioned spending her twenties locked up in a psychiatric hospital, but there she is. Stuck with bad food, rude staff, and rules, rules, rules. The place is interminably dull. At least, it is until the murders start. Oh, sure, management claims the deaths are accidents, but Iris knows better. How? Because she can speak to the victims.

Newly qualified psychiatrist Marcus Hastings never aspired to work in a secure unit, but his student loans won't pay themselves. And he hates to back away from a challenge, even if that challenge is a delusional blonde who talks to birds, squirrels, and occasionally thin air. Fascinating, in a purely clinical sense, of course.

When fate throws them together, will Iris escape with her life? And will Marcus escape with his sanity?

For more details: www.elise-noble.com/demented

The next Blackwood book will be *Nickel*, in the Blackwood Elements series, releasing in 2020.

Nickel

When Sloane Mullins catches her boyfriend in a compromising position with another woman, her meddling friend Leah decides that a better model is exactly what Sloane needs, whether she wants to start dating again or not.

Meanwhile, colleague Logan steps in to rescue her from one disaster after another. What if the perfect man has been under her nose the whole time?

For more details: www.elise-noble.com/nickel

If you enjoyed Glitter, please consider leaving a review.

For an author, every review is incredibly important. Not only do they make us feel warm and fuzzy inside, readers consider them when making their decision whether or not to buy a book. Even a line saying you enjoyed the book or what your favourite part was helps a lot.

Want to stalk me?

For updates on my new releases, giveaways, and other random stuff, you can sign up for my newsletter on my website:
www.elise-noble.com

Facebook:
www.facebook.com/EliseNobleAuthor

Twitter: @EliseANoble

Instagram: @elise_noble

If you're on Facebook, you may also like to join Team Blackwood for exclusive giveaways, sneak previews, and book-related chat. Be the first to find out about new stories, and you might even see your name or one of your ideas make it into print!

And if you'd like to read my books for FREE, you can also find details of how to join my review team.

Would you like to join Team Blackwood?

www.elise-noble.com/team-blackwood

END OF BOOK STUFF

Congratulations on reading this book! If you've made it this far, it means you've survived Christmas 2019.

I hope you enjoyed this trip back in time to visit Emmy, Ana, and Bradley—I'd been wondering for a while how Ana got from retiring at the end of Ultraviolet to shooting people again, and now I know, lol. This is one of the fun things about being a writer—I can go back and fill in the gaps. While I was putting the finishing touches to Glitter, I had a fun idea for my next "between the numbers" novella, which involves Emmy, Dan, Bradley, and Christmas. Somewhat ironic because I'm basically Scrooge McGrinch. My other half and I have already had the "shall we put the tree up this year?" conversation and decided that neither of us can be bothered because we'll only have to take it down again.

So, how does December look in the Noble household? Well, this year, I'm fostering an epileptic rescue dog while writing, Netflixing (is that a word?), and gorging myself on party food. Luckily, having the pupper gives me a great excuse not to actually *go* to parties #Introvert. The only time I set foot outside is to walk the dogs or cater to Trev's whims because I was definitely born on the wrong continent and therefore wasn't designed to do winter.

What about books in 2020? It's half planned... First up will be *Demented*, the fourth instalment of the Electi series. Then *Nickel*, Sloane and Logan's story in the Elements series. For sure there'll be some Blackwood Security books—Alaric's story was going to be one book, then two, and now it's three, each with a sub-story sort of like the Black Trilogy. I've also got a little paranormal standalone to squeeze in somewhere, plus a new series to release into the wild. And Club Dead to finish, plus the aforementioned Christmas novella to write, and... Yeah, it's gonna be a busy year.

Guess I'd better get started...

Hope you have a fantastic 2020,

Elise

OTHER BOOKS BY ELISE NOBLE

The Blackwood Security Series
For the Love of Animals (Nate & Carmen - prequel)
Black is my Heart (prequel)
Pitch Black
Into the Black
Forever Black
Gold Rush
Gray is my Heart
Neon (novella)
Out of the Blue
Ultraviolet
Glitter (novella)
Red Alert
White Hot
The Scarlet Affair
Quicksilver
The Girl with the Emerald Ring (2020)
Red After Dark (2020)
When the Shadows Fall (2020)

The Blackwood Elements Series
Oxygen
Lithium
Carbon
Rhodium

Platinum
Lead
Copper
Bronze
Nickel (2020)

The Blackwood UK Series
Joker in the Pack
Cherry on Top (novella)
Roses are Dead
Shallow Graves
Indigo Rain
Pass the Parcel (TBA)

Blackwood Casefiles
Stolen Hearts

Blackstone House
Hard Lines (TBA)
Hard Tide (TBA)

The Electi Series
Cursed
Spooked
Possessed
Demented (2020)

The Trouble Series
Trouble in Paradise
Nothing but Trouble
24 Hours of Trouble

Standalone

Life
Twisted (short stories)
A Very Happy Christmas (novella)